Maple is on a mission.

Dear Dawn and Beetle,

    I left to go and find the Wise Woman. I am not trying to make trouble. I just need to help the baby. I will find the fountain and bring water back. I will be home today by sundown and we can go to the hospital and bring the water to the baby. Please don't worry, because Papa has taught me a lot about being out in the woods and please don't tell Gramma I have gone. I don't want her worrying. Tell her I went on a walk or that I am playing in my room. You'll think of something.

                    Love, your sister

                    Maple T. Rittle

OTHER BOOKS YOU MAY ENJOY

flutter

THE STORY OF FOUR SISTERS
AND
ONE INCREDIBLE JOURNEY

ERIN E. MOULTON

PUFFIN BOOKS
An Imprint of Penguin Group (USA) Inc.

PUFFIN BOOKS

Published by the Penguin Group

Penguin Young Readers Group, 345 Hudson Street, New York, New York 10014, U.S.A.

Penguin Group (Canada), 90 Eglinton Avenue East, Suite 700, Toronto, Ontario, Canada M4P 2Y3
(a division of Pearson Penguin Canada Inc.)

Penguin Books Ltd, 80 Strand, London WC2R 0RL, England

Penguin Ireland, 25 St Stephen's Green, Dublin 2, Ireland (a division of Penguin Books Ltd)

Penguin Group (Australia), 250 Camberwell Road, Camberwell, Victoria 3124, Australia
(a division of Pearson Australia Group Pty Ltd)

Penguin Books India Pvt Ltd, 11 Community Centre,
Panchsheel Park, New Delhi - 110 017, India

Penguin Group (NZ), 67 Apollo Drive, Rosedale, Auckland 0632, New Zealand
(a division of Pearson New Zealand Ltd.)

Penguin Books (South Africa) (Pty) Ltd, 24 Sturdee Avenue,
Rosebank, Johannesburg 2196, South Africa

Registered Offices: Penguin Books Ltd, 80 Strand, London WC2R 0RL, England

First published in the United States of America by Philomel Books,
a division of Penguin Young Readers Group, 2011
Published by Puffin Books, a division of Penguin Young Readers Group, 2012

1 3 5 7 9 10 8 6 4 2

Copyright © Erin E. Robinson, 2011

THE LIBRARY OF CONGRESS HAS CATALOGED THE PHILOMEL BOOKS EDITION AS FOLLOWS:
Moulton, Erin E.
Flutter: the story of four sisters and one incredible journey / Erin E. Moulton.
p. cm.
Summary: Nine-and-a-half-year-old Maple and her older sister, Dawn, must work together
to face treacherous terrain, wild animals, and poachers as they trek through Vermont's
Green Mountains seeking a miracle for their prematurely-born sister.
ISBN: 978-0-399-25515-1 (hc)
[1. Sisters—Fiction. 2. Adventure and adventurers—Fiction. 3. Nature—Fiction.
4. Poaching—Fiction. 5. Family life—Vermont—Fiction. 6. Vermont—Fiction.]
I. Title.
PZ7.M8593Flu 2011
[Fic]—dc22   2010014507

Puffin Books ISBN 978-0-14-242133-8

Edited by Jill Santopolo   Design by Semadar Megged

Text set in 11-Point Village

Printed in the United States of America

For my sisters, who remain beautiful, smart, and strong.

flutter

Chapter One

It all starts at home. On the mountain. Three miles up a rutted dirt road, out past Mr. Benny's apple orchard and over the hill from Nanny Ann's farm stand. It's fall now, my favorite season. And in just a few days, we are going to be having my favorite holiday: Halloween. Yep, out here on Canton Creek Turnpike, it's time for candy collecting and pumpkin carving.

Papa's prepping my pumpkin, and I am looking out the window. The sun has almost set, leaving the world soaked in streaks of orange and heavy purple shadows. It's the best time of day, with everything turning gold.

The swing set, the river, and the already fallen leaves melt together in the dusk. Our ox, Millament, is walking lazily toward the barn. Going to get warm, I suppose. I bet he wishes he was in here, and I sorta do too. The fire is crackling in the woodstove and the house is alive with noises: Mama humming in the kitchen, sisters fussing around the table, and Papa slicing away at the top of that pumpkin.

I'm about to come away from the window and get started, but then a little glimmer of brown flits in and out of the shadows and for a minute it looks like a leaf tumbling in the wind, out of control, but then it lands just below the window and I can see it's a genuine monarch butterfly. I put my hands up to the glass because that monarch is crazy to be out there this time of year. She wouldn't have the proper amount of meat on her bones to survive. I'm breathing quick and thinking maybe I had better go and get it to come inside, but I fog up the window with my breath and when the fog disappears, the monarch's gone. I hope it's headed south and not trying to prove it can make it through the winter.

"There you are, kiddo. Get started," Papa says.

I turn toward him. He wipes his hands off on a kitchen towel.

I go over to the table and pull the top off the pumpkin. I put it down next to me. I am about to dip my hand into the mushy insides when Beetle, my little sister, comes running around the corner of the counter. She holds a small gourd to her belly, then she teeters and totters to the edge of the table and throws it on the floor. It thuds but doesn't crack. She squeals with glee and picks it up again. This time, she heads straight for our mutt, Curious, who snoozes by the woodstove. Not for long, though. A second later, Beetle drops the gourd right next to Curious and he lifts his head and stares at her with a what-do-you-think-you-are-doing look. Curious and I are genuine friends, so we have good eye communication, and I can tell he wants this business to stop right now so he can relax.

"Come on, Beetle, don't bug Curio," I say. She picks the gourd up and carries it to me. She'll probably start drooling on my leg or something, 'cause that is what babies do. They don't have control of all their body yet. She hangs on to my leg, and I pat her on the head and look across the table.

Dawn, my older sister, sets down her knife. She's all done; her pumpkin has been gutted and carved. It stares at me meanly.

"Don't copy mine, Maple," she says.

Like I would want to copy hers anyway. I am going to make a real masterpiece. Dawn wipes her hands and opens her book. It's a journal, and Dawn writes all her thoughts in it. I've read almost all of them. There is a little spot behind the bottom drawer in her desk. She puts it back there where she thinks no one can find it. But I know it's there, and sometimes candies are there too, which I like just as well. I haven't read any of it this whole week, so I peer with eyelids almost shut at her book. That way she doesn't know I'm looking.

*Trevor Collins is the worst kid in my class. Just because your dad is the park ranger doesn't mean you know everything there is to know about the woods. We went outside yesterday and he—*Dawn slams her forearm across the entry just as I start getting involved.

"Quit looking at my paper and carve your pumpkin, Maple," she says.

I sit back in my chair and ignore her glare. I think about carving the best pumpkin in town. Two days before Halloween, the Bee's Nest, our general store, empties out its parking lot of all the cars and sets up big pumpkin stands. Everyone in town brings a pumpkin. The whole place seems to glow orange, and some of the pumpkins are real amazing. Last year, there was one with the town center on it. I figure I will try something like that. I dig my hand into the pumpkin's belly and start loosening the seeds. You have to really pull to get them all out, and you have to dig around with the top of a mason jar to clean it proper.

Papa sits at the end of the table and puts his glasses on his nose. He flips through a worn-out field guide called *Birds of the Northeast.* He looks up and says, "And the Latin name of the cardinal is—"

I plop some seeds into a bowl of water in the middle of the kitchen table, and Dawn and I say, "*Cardinalis cardinalis.*" Of course, that one's a cinch. They aren't all that easy, but I've memorized a bunch of them so far. Papa makes us learn a new one every Sunday. Other nights of the week we review the ones we already know.

I dig my hand in again and chuck some pumpkin seeds into the bowl. This time, a little bit splashes out accidentally and lands right on Dawn's page.

"Maple!" Dawn's face gets red, and she jumps up and starts dabbing at it with some newspaper.

"Jeez Louise, I didn't mean—" I start to say, but she picks up her journal and walks to the other end of the table, near Papa. He doesn't look up. He just keeps flipping the pages of his book. He's pretty involved.

"Mama, did you see what Maple did?" Dawn turns and holds her book up to the light.

"It'll dry, Dawn. You know it was an accident," Mama says, and I smile inwardly knowing Mama's on my side. I look over at her where she stands in the kitchen, her apron dusted in flour. She is making something that smells real good. I think it's going to be sticky and sweet and covered in frosting that I can lick off the tips of my fingers. She slaps some dough on the counter and looks at me.

"Do you want to come and help me work the dough?" she asks.

I toss some more pumpkin seeds into the bowl and wipe my hands off on my shirt. Mama grimaces. I come around the counter and she has already got a stool out for me to stand on. I step up onto it in front of her. Her arms come around me and I can feel her big belly and the new baby kicking inside. Mama says babies grow the best when they know that there are good things waiting on the outside for them, so we have to be supportive of it and talk to it a lot. I rub it and feel it under Mama's skin.

"Time to make the dough, baby," I say. Then I spin around to help Mama.

"Just like this," Mama says, and she pushes her palm into the dough. Then she lets me have a try. The flour is soft on my hands, but soon the dough gets stickier and we have to add more. Mama sprinkles the flour down and sings in my ear.

> *From the sky she fell*
> *Softly in the trees.*
> *If you gather round I'll tell*
> *Of Old Lady Hope, you'll see.*

FLUTTER 7

> Old Lady Hope will soothe,
> Wise Woman of the Mountains.
> When wind and rain and sleet do swell
> Collect water from her fountain.
> Pure waters from the mountain.

Mama's been teaching me this song one verse at a time and I am to the point where I know nearly the whole thing. I thump the dough with my palms and pitch in my voice too. I can feel the singing from the tips of my toes to the tips of my fingers.

> Seek her out in times of plight
> When you don't know where to start.
> She is where the answer lies
> Follow with your heart.

"Mayel," Beetle says. I didn't even know she had made it all the way over here until I feel the stem of the gourd jab right into my foot.

"Beetle, don't do that," I tell her and kick at her a little bit, but she looks up at me from her spot on the floor and starts giggling like something is hilarious.

I feel Mama laugh and the baby pats my back, but I keep on going, pressing my fingers into that nice soft dough.

Full of water, wind and sun,
Hold your head up high.
Deep within the mountain's song
You will hear her sigh.

Love and love and round we go,
Clasp your hands and sing.
Round and round and round we go
To form the healing ring—

"How's the rest go, Mama?" I say. Mama chimes in with her sugar sweet voice:

Water, sun, moon, and rain
Will do their part to heal.
Still greater powers come to call
When love brings strength, concealed . . .
Love and love, the purest love
He—

"Agh." Dawn slams her book shut. "It's so loud in here. I am going to go light my pumpkin."

I hit the dough some more as Dawn gets her fleece jacket out of the closet. She grabs gloves and picks up her jack-o'-lantern.

"Can I have the lighter, Mama?" she asks as she stands

at the door. And I hope Mama says she cannot have the lighter, but Mama looks over at Papa. He gets up out of his chair.

"I'll come out with you, Dawn. Hang on." Papa grabs Beetle away from my feet and puts a little jacket on her, and then they hurry out onto the porch.

"Mama, can I—" But before I even finish, Mama is wiping my hands off with a washcloth.

"You go ahead, little one," she says.

I run to the closet as fast as I can and get the first coat that touches my fingers. It's one of Papa's red flannel jackets. I shove my arms into the big holes and head out onto the porch with the others. The stars are out and clear as crystal.

Papa lights a candle and passes it to Dawn. "Now just lower it in—"

"I've done this before, Papa," Dawn says and lowers the candle into the grinning jack-o'-lantern. Once the candle settles, she puts the cap back on sideways. I can smell wax and burning pumpkin. An orange glow lights our faces and hands, and I step a little closer to get some warmth on my fingers.

Papa stands up tall like he is listening real close, so I put my head up too and search with my ears. I hear something far off. It's nothing but a whine at first, then it gets bigger and bigger. Coyotes! Lots of them.

One minute we listen, and then my papa fills his lungs full and lets out a howl straight into the night sky. It's so cold his breath puffs out in a long billowing line. I'm thinking it's crazy for a minute, then I set in too. I don't know why, but it's the best feeling when you're screaming into the sky and you're not sure if it's your own voice coming back at you or someone or something else answering your call. Beetle starts waving her hand in the air and tries to make the sound, but she's one and a half, and she hasn't got it quite right yet. She sounds more like that annoying dog at Mr. Machetee's, just down the road. Dawn is two years older than me. She's eleven and a half, and I think she might be getting too old for this howling, because she keeps rolling her eyes and sighing.

Anyway, there we are howling, and my voice, or something, is flying right back in my face when Curious starts making a big fuss indoors. I catch a glimpse of him in the bay window. He's got his nose up against the glass and it's smearing and smudging and his paw is up and scratching. I've seen him do this before, but something is different about it. His ears are all perked up, and his eyes are going wild this way and that.

Then I hear a big crash, and Papa is running inside so fast you wouldn't believe it. Beetle bounces up and down in his arms and, of course, starts to bawl. Papa hugs her to his chest and runs out of sight. We are out on the porch, Dawn and I. Dawn just looks at me and the coyotes yip and yap, and Curious barks and scrambles, and I hear Papa's steps pound up and down and all around the house.

All of a sudden, everything is still for a moment, and then I hear Mama. I hear my mama like her voice is coming through a long tunnel, and it starts out as a slow quiet moan and then it gets louder and louder. I run before I even find my legs, because I look straight into Dawn's eyes and I can be sure something is really wrong. I can be sure nothing has been so wrong in my entire life. Dawn darts in front of me. The bottoms of her shoes flash like the white velvet of a deer tail.

I run through that door, and there is Beetle on the floor crying next to my mama who is also on the floor crying. Her belly pops up like a huge balloon. Papa has got Mama's face in his hand and he looks down at her and talks quiet and breathes fast. Seeing everything so abrupt like this makes my knees start to shake, and I'm not sure what to do. I'm breathing fast from running, and my hands flap and my toes curl and my heart hits my chest like a woodpecker on a birch tree.

My papa talks to me, but I can't hear him above the pounding. His mouth moves and his eyebrows come down in the middle and, well, he says something, see, but I don't do anything 'cause I'm not sure what's going on. But Dawn listens and she can hear something and she runs into the other room and she's got the phone in her hand. I have Beetle in my lap now, and I try to calm her down 'cause tears are coming down her cheeks like raindrops in April. I pat back her curls and kiss her on the angel kiss on her head.

From my spot on the floor I can see my mama's face real close. It's scrunched up, like when she is mad, but there is something else there. I grab her fingers, which are white and dusty from flour.

"What's the matter, Mama?" I ask.

"Nothing, baby. It's nothing. Just pregnancy pains," she says. She gives my hand a squeeze and tears roll out of her eyes and mine too. I put my hand on Mama's belly to see how the baby is doing. *Thump thump*, little feet kick against my palm. *It's not time yet*, I think. I rub her belly and try to make it calm, but something shudders and patters against my fingertips, my thumb. The thumping grows lighter, softer, weaker. *What is it?* I think. I put my ear down to hear. The sound is hollow when I close my ear on Mama's stomach. *BompBompBompBomp*, HelpHelpHelpHelp. Help. *I'm listening*, I think, but hands grip me below my armpits. They pull me to my feet.

"Wait," I say, but strangers have ahold of me, and my voice gets stuck inside of me. They turn me around, and the room tilts and twirls. They push me out. But I stand at the edge of the living room and crouch down so I can peek around the corner of the sofa.

Papa takes Beetle and holds her to his chest. His face is wet with tears, and he talks to the people who walk into my house. They've come with a rolling bed and a loud truck. Everyone rushes around. The people in uniform stomp on the floor and push things out of the way. A chair knocks against the table and my half-gutted pumpkin teeters and rolls onto its side, spilling a gob of seeds across the kitchen table. Dawn is crying, and Beetle is screaming and Mama is huffing like she is having a hard time catching her breath. Before I realize it, my legs are taking me straight out of there. They take me up the stairs and into my rosy room. Only it isn't so rosy. The lights are bouncing off the walls, making everything blue and red, and the colors fill my eyes.

I peer out the window, and I see them roll Mama along the driveway and into the back of a truck. I don't know if it is my imagination or what, but all of a sudden my attention goes to the screen right in front of my face. A set of wings is beating and battering at my window. They flutter sporadically and I am frozen stock-still wondering what the heck it is. It being dark and the end of autumn, reason would tell me it's a bat. But I am looking at it, and it's much too small to be a bat, doesn't have enough flutter to be a moth. That means it's only one thing. A butterfly. All I know is something must be really wrong if nature isn't acting the way it ought to.

My throat tightens up and I am not sure, but it's awful hot in here for such a cool autumn night. Those butterfly wings change from blue to red, back and forth they flicker. My feet start jumping and I turn and run. I grab Paddington Bear right off my bed, head straight to the linen closet and scoot myself in among the soft sheets.

There are no lights here. The screaming of the siren is less, and I can hear my own breathing. The sheets, they smell like comfort. Fresh and clean. I wrap myself up in them. Then the tears come again, and all I can think of is the baby fluttering there in Mama's stomach, scared. My palm tingles and I picture baby footprints imprinted on my hand. I hear her cry in my head. *BompBompBompBomp,* HelpHelpHelpHelp.

Chapter Two

I'm awake. I'm in my bed. It must have been a dream. The last thing I remember is the closet, and here I am in my rosy room. The sun shines through my window, and I hear my favorite band, Creedence Clearwater Revival, spinning on the record player.

I sing along as Curious stretches in the sun spot on the floor. He's not supposed to be up here, but I love it when he is.

"C'mon, boy," I say as I throw off my blankets and smack my feet right into the rug. Curious jumps up. He does a shake and stretch and I give his chin a scrub with my fingernails.

We head out the door and down the stairs. I stop
halfway down and grab Curious real quick by the collar.
He tries to get down in front of me, but I'm stuck in my
spot 'cause there is something going on. I peek my head
over the banister lightning fast and dive back down.

Gramma.

What's she doing here?

I peek my head up over the banister again and continue my investigation. She's biting her nails, and her
eyes look kind of swollen up like she's been crying all
night. She's got the phone up to her ear and now she
hits her head with her palm. My legs are ahead of me
as I pull Curious, and we are going back up the stairs.
Beetle plays with Lincoln Logs on the floor and Dawn
walks out of her room, rubbing her eyes. She makes a
beeline for the stairs. I grab her arm and put my finger to
my lips. She scowls, but I can tell she's with me. I point
toward the phone. We tiptoe, just in case our steps give
away our location. I lift as Dawn places her finger on the
receiver.

"—complications." My papa, but his voice sounds
small, somehow.

"What does that mean? There were complications?"
My gramma, high-pitched, frantic.

Dawn's eyes are wide as we listen, and my stomach
is in knots.

"The baby, she's weak, small. She doesn't have a whole lot of life in her. I'm praying for a miracle—" My ears begin to buzz.

Dawn rips the phone out of my hand and rests it in the cradle. All the visions of last night tumble through my mind like mountain lions caught in a wrestling match. I lick my lips. Once. Twice. Three times.

"We have a sister. We have a new baby sister, but, but—" Dawn whispers. Dawn falls on her knees and she's crying. My tongue is stuck still like a stick in the mud, and my throat feels like it is caving in on itself. In the end, my voice escapes in a wild scream. Once I start, Beetle joins in too. Eyes streaming, nose running.

And then Gramma's here. She plucks up Beetle and kisses her on the cheek.

"C'mon, girls, let's go downstairs and have some tea. I want to talk to you about something." She shifts Beetle to one arm and reaches way down and then her soft wrinkly hand is holding mine.

"Rest that voice for just a minute, chicken," she says, rubbing her thumb back and forth across my knuckles.

My legs have a hard time moving, but Gramma tugs on my hand. *Move*, I think, *don't make trouble*. I drop Gramma's hand real fast.

"Just a minute!" I say. I run into my room, pull Paddington off the bed and am down the stairs fast.

In the living room, we pile onto the couch like baby mice trying to keep warm and safe. I know they do this because we found a mess of 'em in the hollow of a tree one time. That's what Papa told me. He said they snuggle up like that to keep themselves warm and safe. So there we are, piled on the couch, Dawn and me up close and Beetle tucked in between. Paddington is there too.

"Girls, listen to me now," Gramma says as she sets a tray on the table. It has a teapot and two mugs on it.

"I know you're scared about what happened last night. But everything is going to be all right." Gramma pours some tea into a Strawberry Shortcake mug and scoops a heaping teaspoon of sugar into it. She stirs quickly and the tea spills out the sides. The brown liquid slides down Strawberry's face.

"Your mama had a new baby this morning. A sister for the three of you. Lily Anne. She's decided to come early, which means she's a little bit small for her age. They're gonna stay in the hospital so that she can be monitored. You're going to go and visit soon—"

"Is she dying?" Dawn nearly shouts this and I think about socking her in the jaw for saying it. Then she whispers, "The baby, Lily, is she dying?"

Gramma swallows hard and lifts her chin. I do the same.

"Come now, Dawn, why would you think a thing

like that?" Gramma drops the spoon and clasps her hands together. Now she pushes her cheeks with the tips of her fingers, and that's a nervous habit I have seen her do before. She crouches down to our level. She smells like baby powder and sugar cookies. She reaches toward us and takes Dawn's hand.

"Lily is . . . is doing . . . well, she's doing okay. And the most important thing that you can do right now is to keep your chin up and get things ready for when she comes home."

She lets go and I look at her. She's not telling the truth. Papa said he is praying for a miracle. Things aren't all right if you have to pray for a miracle. Gramma gets up and goes into the kitchen.

Dawn slouches on the armrest and I see Gramma putting dishes away in the cupboards. She starts to hum a little, and before I think twice, I realize I am humming too. Only it's a different song. It's the song Mama is teaching me.

> Old Lady Hope will soothe,
> Wise Woman of the Mountains.
> When wind and rain and sleet do swell
> Collect water from her fountain.
> Pure waters from the mountain.
> Seek her out in times of plight

When you don't know where to start.
She is where the answer lies—

And then it's like a bright light pops on right inside my head. I start remembering the tale of Old Lady Hope, the Wise Woman of the Mountains. Mama used to tell us the story before we went to bed at night. I'd get all snugged down in the soft sheets and she'd start in:

"Once a long, long time ago, the world held both humans and spirits. There were earth spirits, air spirits, water spirits, and fire spirits. And on top of that, there were light spirits. You still see these today, baby. Sometimes walking in the morning grass you'll see light spirits twinkling in the dew. The light spirits were the ones with the greatest healing power. Old Lady Hope, otherwise known as the Wise Woman of the Mountains, was once a light spirit herself.

"Do you remember when we went outside and watched the colors dancing in the sky? That, Maple, is called the aurora borealis, or the northern lights. When the Wise Woman of the Mountains was a light spirit, she was the strongest, most healing kind; she was part of the aurora borealis. But, Maple, she didn't like her place in the sky. She looked down on the earth and saw all of the people here. She saw that people suffered, and she saw their sorrowful eyes peer up at her every once in a while. And to be sure, she knew that they were soothed, but she longed to help them more. So after looking down for many years she decided it was time, and she slipped straight out of heaven and fell in the woods of the Green Mountains. She struck the earth with such force that she and earth joined. They erupted together into a towering rock. She felt her essence and her healing power strengthen, and she cried tears of joy. These tears collected in a pool below her. Soon, the natives of Vermont, and the settlers after them, found her there. They learned that a visit to the Wise Woman meant that they could be cured of every ill. They visited her often. She loved the company and felt whole, for she was able to help them so.

"She still stands there today, Maple, and as times and beliefs change, she is visited less and less by people, and more and more by the woodland creatures. But some say she still has those healing powers. That she still grants miracles. All you have to say is:

> *Please, Wise Woman*
> *Have mercy on me.*
> *Grant me a miracle*
> *If pure my soul be.*
> *Grant me this wish,*
> *I ask of you.*

Grant me this wish
My intention is true."

Mama would stroke my hair back from my face and say, "Then simply collect the water, hold it fast, and read the inscription that lies at the bottom of the pool. Do these things, and you will have your miracle."

I am certain that if anyone can grant a miracle, it's the Wise Woman of the Mountains. I just have to find out where she is, how to get to her.

I wait till Gramma comes back in from the kitchen. She yawns a big yawn and puts on the TV set. Then she sits in the recliner and pulls a pair of knitting needles out of a basket.

"I have to run to the bathroom," I say.

Gramma nods, and I get up and walk straight for the bathroom, only when I get to Papa's office I take a sharp right and open the door real quiet. I know I am not supposed to be in here without Papa, but I know that he wouldn't mind me being in here if he knew what an emergency it was. I slide through and leave the door open just a crack. I spin and move past Papa's desk and the sap bucket filled with maps. I stand tiptoe on the wood floor and crane my neck to the top shelf of books. I'm trying to think up the title from my memory, but I just can't seem to find it. It's something to do with mountains and stories or folklore or something. I scan one shelf and then the next, but nothing refreshes my memory.

I hear footsteps behind me, then a squeaky little baby voice says, "Sa!"

Great. I wheel around and sure enough Beetle and Dawn are standing in the doorway.

"What are you doing in here?" Dawn whispers as she tiptoes in. Beetle hangs on to Dawn's hand as I motion them close.

"Where is Gramma?" I ask, worrying she will come through the door any second.

"I told her I had to go and get something," Dawn says. "What's going on? What are you doing in here?"

I don't really want to tell her, but I know she'll be able to help me find the book I'm looking for. Scholars are good at remembering and retrieving information, and Dawn is a scholar if I ever saw one.

"I'm looking for the book about Green Mountain folk-lore or legends or something. You know, the one that has the Wise Woman of the Mountains in it?"

Dawn squints her eyes up for a minute.

"Why are you looking for that book?" she asks me.

"I need some information out of it," I say.

"I'm not telling you the title unless you tell me why you need it," she says.

Figures she is going to be stubborn right at the worst time.

Beetle bounces around like she is listening to music, and she starts to tug on Dawn's hand. I know we're going to get caught 'cause Beetle is being a little bit too loud.

"I need some information about where the Wise Woman is located . . . for a research project . . . for school," I lie.

Dawn stares at me like she is trying to read my thoughts. "It's *Mountain Legends*," she says and pulls Beetle past me to the bookshelf. She scans at head height, and Beetle points at the books and nods.

"They're in alphabetical order," Dawn says. "The A's are up at the top, so it must be somewhere around—"

My heart jumps straight into my throat as Gramma's voice calls us from the other room. "Girls! Girls, where are you?"

Beetle hears Gramma and lets go of Dawn's hand. She starts to teeter toward the door.

"No you don't," I whisper and grab her chubby little fist. She starts to tug, and I see her face scrunching into a frown. "C'mon, Dawn," I say, clenching my teeth.

Dawn scans the titles faster. Her hand shushes along one row and then another.

"No, sisa," Beetle whines and squirms.

"Shhhh . . ." I say, but babies don't really get sneakiness, so she just keeps on squirming.

"Oh, it must be in alphabetical order by name," Dawn says, and clicks her fingernails on her teeth.

I am sifting through all the names I can think of—Jones, Thompson, Arbuckle, Paterson—but I just don't remember the name of the person who wrote that book.

"It's Kendall." Her fingers slide across the K section. "Nope."

Beetle drops to her butt and starts kicking at me with fierce legs.

"You have to hurry. Gramma is looking for us," I say.

"Don't rush me or I won't remember it at all."

It feels like it takes her half an hour, but finally she says, "It must be Perkinson." She starts scanning the P's.

Then Beetle lets out a loud giggle and starts crawling for Papa's desk chair. I reach to grab her, but she sees a compass hanging from a hook and heads toward it. She's faster than a free-range chicken.

"Ohhh, Beetle, quiet now, come to Maple," I whisper, like it is going to make up for all the noise she is making.

"Ahh, here it is."

I spin toward Dawn. I can see the corner of the book despite her trying to hide it behind her back.

"Now, are you going to tell me why you are looking for this book?" she asks.

"I told you, I need it for a research project," I whisper.

"Maple, are you telling me the truth? I heard you singing just before you came in here, that song that Mama has been teaching you. I know that story inside and out, and I can tell you for a fact that it is folklore. You're not thinking anything stupid, are you?"

"No." I go toward her, trying to judge whether I will be fast enough.

"Good, because you know it's just a story, Maple," she says.

"Give me the book," I say, diving after it. We both slam into the bookshelf as Gramma walks in.

"There you kids are," Gramma says. She frowns when she sees us smashed up against the shelf. Dawn is holding the book just out of my reach.

"You know you're not supposed to be in here when your papa isn't with you," Gramma says and reaches down to pick up Beetle, who has made her way around the desk and is almost out the door.

"Sorry, Gramma. We were looking for a book to read," I say.

"Well, there are plenty of books in your room and in Dawn's room. Why don't we go and look for a good one and then rustle up some lunch?"

She slides the door open for us to walk out. Dawn puts the book back where it was. I keep my eye on it and record the information to memory: second shelf, near the middle. No one is gonna stop me now.

Chapter Three

Gramma keeps us busy for the entire day. We read books and play games. We play Candy Land, Chutes and Ladders, Cherry-O, and Jenga, but I don't have one single bit of fun. I try to sneak back into Papa's office, but every time I do either Gramma is eyeing me, or Dawn is ready to blurt out what I am about to do. I see her crossing her arms and glaring at me. She says that we have to listen to Gramma, that the doctors will be able to take care of the baby. But they don't seem to be doing that so far. There hasn't been any good news from the hospital. Lily needs a genuine miracle. So, like always, I'm on my own.

I write the letter before I go to bed. Mr. Crock says I am the best writer in my class, so I scribble the words down careful and sincere:

Dear Dawn and Beetle,

> *I left to go and find the Wise Woman. I am not trying to make trouble. I just need to help the baby. I will find the fountain and bring water back. I will be home today by sundown and we can go to the hospital and bring the water to the baby. Please don't worry, because Papa has taught me a lot about being out in the woods and please don't tell Gramma I have gone. I don't want her worrying. Tell her I went on a walk or that I am playing in my room. You'll think of something.*

> *Love, your sister*
> *Maple T. Rittle*

I jam the note into a pocket of my pants, which I fold and pile under my pillow. I pull a napkin filled with leftover dinner—kielbasa and cabbage—out of my right pocket, grab a cookie from my other pocket and throw them all into a red handkerchief. I tie all four corners into a knot. I slide open the front pocket of my backpack and jam the food into one of my sneakers. Then I go over to my bookshelf. In the back, behind *Adventures of Huckleberry Finn,* is where I hide my emergency gear. I keep these things just in case any of us get into a big fight and I have to get out of here. And boy, am I glad that I put up the extra effort. I pull the book out and there is a can of maple-glazed baked beans. Yum. Next to the can, in a little Ziploc bag, is my emergency fire-starting kit. I pull both of these out and shove them in with my sneakers. Then I double-check my supplies. I have an emergency meal. A Maglite for later tonight. One empty bottle to collect the miracle water, and one bottle full of water to keep me hydrated. I had to be a sneak and fill it up in the bathroom sink, but I figure bathroom water is better than none at all.

I also have a winter coat, 'cause I can tell already it'll be freezing cold until the sun rises. The coat barely fits into the bag, so I smoosh it down with an elbow and zip with the opposite hand.

Just like Huck, I am good to go. I push my backpack into the dark under my bed, and while I am down there, I pull out a box labeled THINKING CAPS. These are genuine thinking caps for Rittle Sister Thinking Meetings. There's one for each sister. Dawn has a top hat. Beetle has a war helmet, and I have a real catamount paw hat. It has a string around the bottom to hold it on, and it came

from a real live catamount. I figure I could use all the
smarts and courage I can find, so I pull the paw hat out
of the box and snug it under my pillow. Then I pull on
my tie-dyed T-shirt that I made at Brookside Camp last
summer. We did lots of outdoor things at Brookside and
I figure this shirt will get me in the mood to be in the
woods. I can basically still smell campfire smoke on it.
I climb under my covers. I set my alarm for three A.M.,
put the volume down low, and put it under Paddington
Bear.

Curious comes into my room, collar jangling, jumps
up on my bed, and curls up in a ball next to my feet.
When I give him a good itch behind his right ear, I notice my hands are a little bit shaky.

"How are we doing, chicken?" Gramma says from the
doorway.

I swallow hard. "Doing okay, I guess."

She comes in and sits on the edge of my bed. She
sees Curious.

"Now, what is he doing up here? He knows he's supposed to sleep downstairs."

She pats him on the head, and he puts a paw on her
leg. Curious is a real good negotiator. "Well, I guess he
can sleep here just for tonight," she says.

"Thanks, Gramma," I say. "I've had a rough day."

She gives me a kiss on my forehead and pats my hair.

"I know, Maple, it has been a rough day for all of us.

But I am confident we will be looking at a brighter day tomorrow." Gramma has twinkly eyes and her hands are soft as they brush down my hair and onto my cheek.

"You have sweet dreams, okay?" She gives me an extra hug and tucks my blanket up around my neck. I feel the alarm clock slide against my arm and I hold my breath, praying that she won't notice the cord snaking toward the outlet. She reaches over and flicks my bedside lamp off. The room pitches into darkness.

"Night, Gramma," I say. "I love you."

"Night, little one. I love you too." And she closes the door, but I appreciate that she leaves it open a crack so that some light from downstairs leaks in. I listen to the yap of coyotes off in the distance. I glance out at the night sky, filled with stars, and think of Lily. I rest my cheek on the palm of my hand. "Don't worry. I'm on my way," I whisper into the shadows. I flip over. Curious snuggles into my feet, and we fall straight asleep.

I jolt up in bed. Voices are wailing, "Bad, Bad Leroy Brown." Curious is up and rustling around with his nose in the covers. My head clears like the sky after a rainstorm. I reach into my sheets until my hand hits the hard plastic. I pull the alarm clock out. Three A.M. It tips and tosses as I try to steady myself. I must have turned the volume up in my sleep. My fingers fumble over plastic buttons and knobs. I hit every one. "Baddest man in the whole—" It goes silent. I stop dead and listen. Someone must have heard it. I count to ten, waiting for Gramma's footsteps, for Beetle's cry, for Dawn's holler from the other room. Nothing but outside noises.

It's kind of light for the middle of the night. The moon has planted a shadow of my window frame onto the rug, but I still wish it was the sun coming in my window instead. Curious crawls up the bed toward me on his belly and licks me straight across the face. I push him off and put my finger to my lips.

"Got to be quiet, Curio, can't let anyone know we're going."

I climb out of bed, reach under my pillow and pull my clothes out. My skin aches with goose bumps; it's not particularly cold, but the house is awake with shadows and whispers. I stand in the moonlight and put my pants on one leg at a time. "Easy, easy, easy," I whisper over and over. I pull on a hooded sweatshirt over my T-shirt. I take my catamount paw hat and secure the strap down under my chin.

I cringe and reach into the darkness under my bed. My hand searches the carpet until it finally touches the strap of my bag. I give it a tug, but the bag won't budge. It's snug in there. I grab the strap and hunker down low in a sorta squat and pull hard. It pops free, and my elbow hits the bookshelf. Pain shoots between my elbow and shoulder. I clamp a hand over my mouth to shut in a scream. Screaming would just about spoil the whole thing. I wipe the stingy tears from my eyes and muster up my courage.

I can barely make out Paddington's shape in the bed. I can't see his eyes or his expression, but something is telling me that he wants to come along.

"Oh, all right," I whisper and pick him up in the crook of my arm. "But you have to fend for yourself. I am not going to be able to do everything for you."

He seems to understand, so I lift my backpack onto my shoulder. I turn toward the doorway. It's still open a crack, but there is no light from downstairs peeking through. It's pitch-dark. "Don't be afraid of that," I tell Paddington. "It's just a little dark. It's exactly the same house as it is during the day."

I feel in front of my face for objects, and feel with my feet for toys that have been left behind. Dawn's room is right across from mine and I breathe a sigh of relief when I see her door is shut. I put my ear up close to the wood to listen for movement. I don't hear anything except for a long steady snore. I pull the note from my pocket and slide it under her door so it will be right in her path when she goes down to breakfast.

I pull myself up. The hallway is long and dark. I put my hand against the wall. I put one foot down, heel first, then toes. I'm quiet, treading like a fox. I reach the top of the stairs. They stretch down into shadows. Paddington is shivering in the crook of my arm.

Curious stands up from where he is sitting and starts down the stairs like it is daybreak. His collar sounds like a million bells splitting the darkness. I spin toward Dawn's door, catching the banister with my right hand, and stop. I stand there a minute, trying to think up an excuse in case she comes out of her room, but nothing happens. When I look again, Curious has disappeared. I step carefully down the stairs. I am walking like I'm on an icy pond, only the ice isn't good and thick. I step down onto the wood floor and stop. The boards creak here, so I pick my leg up real high and make a giant step toward the dining room. I put one foot down, then the next. No sound. I breathe a sigh and put my arm to the wall, heading out toward the bathroom. When I am almost there I turn right and sneak the study door open. I need the book, and the map, so I know where I am going and what exactly I am looking for.

Papa likes fresh air on warm autumn days, and it has been warm this fall, but he forgot to shut the window when he went to the hospital. A cool breeze blows in and lifts a couple of papers from his desk. They twist and turn and fall together on the floor at my feet. A coyote calls in the distance, but the call isn't friendly like the other night. It's not fun, and it's not like the howl Papa makes. The office is cold and full of shadows, and my chest feels like ice. My legs refuse to budge.

Quiet as a catamount, I tell myself. *Quiet as a catamount and as clever as a fox.* I turn away from the window, scared of yellow eyes peering in. I lean up against Papa's desk. The wood is cold on my arm.

"Stay here," I tell Paddington and prop him up next to me.

I wiggle the backpack off my shoulders and dig out my Maglite. I run my hand up the metal to the rubber button and press it on. Gorillas, monsters, and towering buildings grow beyond the beam. But my path is clear. Quiet as a catamount. Clever as a fox. Quiet as a cata-mount. Clever as a fox.

I sweep my flashlight back and forth. The beam pushes the darkness from side to side. What I thought to be a gorilla melts into a fluffy couch, a monster into a fax machine, and buildings into piles of books stacked to fall. *I know this place,* I tell myself. *It is safe.*

The wall of books comes up fast. I slide my finger along the titles. Second shelf. Near the middle. I search over soft covers made of leather, worn scratchy spines made of paper, shiny hard spines that send cold through my fingertips. It takes forever to find the P's.

Finally, my hand comes across a worn hard cover. I have to strain my eyes to make out the letters that are carved into the binding: *Mountain Legends* by Louis Kendall Perkinson.

I slide it off the shelf and wheel around the way I came. "Quiet as a catamount, clever as a fox," I whisper under my breath. I whisper with every step until I reach the sap bucket filled with maps. They stand, jagged-edged and stark white, like bones picked clean. At first I don't even want to touch them, but then I tell myself not to be silly. There is no bucket of bones in Papa's office. I check through the titles. New Hampshire. Maine. Vermont. Washington County, Vermont. Stowe, Vermont. Mooreland, Vermont. I pull out the Mooreland map and tuck it under my arm. I spin the flashlight up and search the wall. The beam lands on Papa's compass. It's in reach of the cold breeze and spins at the end of its leather lanyard. I balance the book, map, and flashlight on one arm and lift the compass off its hook. I slide it over my head and around my neck.

Quiet, quiet, quiet, I tiptoe back toward Papa's desk. A coyote shrieks, and I drop the flashlight straight out of my hand. It hits the floor with a thud and conks out. My mouth goes dry. I lick sweat off my upper lip and wipe my face with the back of my sleeve. For a minute, I am trying to figure out how I am sweating when that window is wide open to the cold night. I shiver. *Don't be a coward, Maple,* I think as I swipe the flashlight up and flick it back on.

Quiet as a catamount. I shuffle my feet along the floor until my toes nudge my backpack. As I pack everything up, I tell myself I'm gonna find a miracle. Gonna save the baby. I lean down and pull my winter jacket out. I pull on one sleeve and then the other. I pull my sneakers out, drop the handkerchief filled with dinner into the backpack, and yank them on. Thank goodness they are Velcro, 'cause I wouldn't be able to hold the flashlight and tie them.

I make sure everything in my backpack is secure. The map stands on end and the paper crinkles as I pull the zipper snug up against it. *Everything is prepared,* I think. *Now all I gotta do is go.* I take a deep breath, adjust my backpack, right my catamount paw on my head, and squeeze Paddington under my arm. "Let's go, old boy," I say. One foot over the next. Low and quiet.

As I look up, something moves. I listen into the dark. I search the shadows. I know I am not alone and that makes my teeth start grinding against each other. I squint toward the window and into the moonlight. No peering yellow eyes. I jerk the flashlight around the study, window to wall to doorway. Coyote? Bear? Mountain lion?

Dawn.

The beam of my flashlight rests on my sister standing

in the doorway. She wears a long nightgown with ruffles on the sleeves. Her eyes are half open and she squints and shields them when I shine the light on her. I see the note in her hand.

"What do you think you're doing?"

"I told you. I am going to find the Wise Woman," I whisper.

"You actually believe that stupid story, don't you?" she says and folds her arms.

"I have to get going," I say.

"I can't let you go. You'll get lost, Maple."

"Maybe, but at least I am willing to do something," I say. I push past her. Curious meets us at the study door and he falls into step by my side.

I peer through the living room, toward the back hall-way, to where Gramma is sleeping in the guest bedroom. Nothing moves. *I'm going to make it,* I think to myself. I tiptoe toward the door. The doorknob is cold to the palm of my hand. I should turn it, but I don't. I hang on and listen to the noises on the other side. Listen to Dawn standing behind me, breathing. *Turn the handle, Maple,* I think to myself. But just as I am about to make my wrist move, Beetle's voice floats down the stairs and, a second later, she starts to cry.

Chapter Four

I dive behind the couch and Dawn's right there next to me. Her nose whistles in my ear and I wave at her that I don't want her stinking breath on the back of my neck. I peer around the opposite side of the couch. Gramma is pushing out of her room and fast. She is in a white nightie, one that looks a lot like what Dawn is wearing. Ruffles and all. I crane my neck. My backpack sits, big as a bear cub, on the other side of the kitchen table where I tried to hide it. I cross my fingers that she won't see it.

She flicks on the living room light and I hear the familiar creak as she moves past the living room to the stairs. I hear Curious's collar jangling. He must be at her heels.

"What are you doing up, boy? Are you master of the house?" Gramma whispers as her footsteps grow quiet.

"Now's my only chance." I try to push past Dawn. But the space between the couch and the wall is tight on this end and she got in last. Paddington and I are penned in like a pair of chickens.

"We need to talk about this, Maple. You can't just go out into the woods in the middle of the night. You'll get eaten," she whispers.

The coyotes are still howling and their screams make my skin prickle with bumps.

A second later, Gramma's footsteps pad down the stairs and Dawn and I duck back down behind the couch. We used to build forts back here, but it doesn't seem nearly as big as it did then.

"Sisa, sisa. Mayel," Beetle whines.

"Poor little chicken. What's the fuss?" I hear Gramma make kissie noises, then, *squish*, she settles into the couch. A lump appears near my face where Gramma is pushing padding through to the other side. I shove Paddington between my back and the wall and nestle into his soft fur. Dawn curls up in a ball. She puts her chin against her knees and stares at the checkered fabric.

Gramma's voice lilts through the house.

Rock-a-bye baby in the treetop
When the wind blows, the cradle will rock
When the bough breaks, the cradle will fall
Down will come baby, cradle and all.

Gramma sings this again and again. And we sit like birds in the snow, tucked in and quiet. But as soon as Gramma stops singing, Curious must realize that we are all awake having a good old time, because his head pops around the corner and he licks Dawn straight across the face. I suck in a gasp, and Dawn wipes her face with her arm.

"Curious, what are you rooting around for back there?" Gramma says, and the lump in the back of the couch shifts a little.

His head jerks up at the sound of his name and he slides backward; his face disappears.

"Finding snacks the girls left? Let me see."

The bump disappears from the back of the couch. We're done for. I close my eyes and pray.

"What is it, boy?" she says.

Curious's collar jangles. I bury my head in my knees.

"Sa! Maaaaaana," Beetle chirps like a little bird. Good old Beetle.

Gramma sighs and the lump appears again.

"What would you like to hear, little chick, would you

like to hear a story? You would? All right," Gramma says, and the couch creaks as she must be rocking Beetle back and forth. "You're restless for your age. That's for sure. Now what story do you want to hear?"

She clucks her tongue a little and all of a sudden I see her hand appear on the windowsill where three pictures sit against the glass. Gramma's hand touches the edges of the picture frames. One is of Dawn, me, and Beetle, one is of Aunt Betty, and one is of Great-Uncle Meyers. She stops on the picture of Great-Uncle Meyers and picks it up off the sill. Her hand and the picture disappear from my view.

"Ahh, do you want to hear about your great-uncle Meyers and the Wise Woman of the Mountains? Now that's a tale."

Dawn shifts and looks over at me, and I shrug my shoulders, telling her that I haven't heard this story before either. Sure, Mama was teaching me the song, and I had heard the original tale of the Wise Woman a gazillion times. But I had never heard this story before.

"The first thing you have to know about your great-uncle Meyers is that he had an old hunting hound named Remington. Remi for short. You would have liked him, little chick, most faithful dog you ever did see. Big drooping eyes, always questioning. And boy did he love your great-uncle Meyers. He never left his side. Wherever

Uncle Meyers was, there was Remi." Gramma's voice is sweet and lulling, and for a minute I stop worrying about the coyotes and settle into the story.

"Your great-uncle had lost almost all his closest kin, so Remi was all the old man had, and he was old when this story takes place. He must have been in his sixties or seventies. Now, given your great-uncle grew up in the woods, he couldn't get it out his head that that was where he belonged. No matter how old he and Remington managed to get, they never stopped taking their hikes out back.

"One morning they walked out past the pines and into the maples. They walked along for a while, crunching through the autumn leaves, and after a couple of hours they came across some mountain lion cubs. You don't see those fellows in this area much these days, little chick, but believe me, they're still out there."

I tug on my catamount paw hat, brush at the fur, 'cause catamounts and mountain lions are one and the same. The feel of the fur helps me zoom in on Gramma's voice and story.

"Well, mark my words, it isn't good to get in the way of the nature of things, and your great-uncle Meyers knew that. He was going to let it all alone. But Remington got curious with his hunting nose and started sticking his head in the den where the litter was holed up. He was in there, pink tongue lolling, licking away at those baby cubs.

"You don't want to see a mama mountain lion mad, little chick. You just don't. She came around the bend fast and saw Remi's tail going wild. She dropped the partridge that was in her mouth and went straight at him. The only thing that saved Remi at that moment was that he was in the den up to his neck. The neck is a very vulnerable spot, little chick, so he was very lucky that she couldn't reach it. But she scratched at his back something fierce and the old hound was sent flying out of that den in real bad shape."

My fingers curl down the side of the hat and land on one of those catamount claws. It still has some sharpness to it, even though it was clipped before it was given to me. Poor Remi, claw marks zigzagging up his back. I don't know what I would do if Curious got attacked. I let go of the claw and tuck my arms in around me.

"Your great-uncle Meyers loved that old dog. Like I said, he would do anything to keep that old hound around. Well, he thought the best thing to do would be to back away. He picked up old Remi quick as he could and put it in reverse. The mama cat didn't go after him. He always claimed that she saw the sorrow in his eyes, but the fact of the matter is, she had given him a warning, and he was backing out of her territory.

"Your great-uncle Meyers carried that old hound for hours, but he wasn't thinking straight with the pup in such poor shape. Remi was hardly breathing, unconscious too. Your great-uncle intended to bring him home and to the vet, but before long he realized he had somehow lost his way. This was strange for your uncle, for he knew those woods like the back of his hand."

My leg is starting to feel all tingly and I try to shift my weight without touching the couch. I wiggle my toes and stretch them wide trying to stop the pins and needles from running up my leg. Gramma just continues through it all.

"Dusk started settling in, little chick, and your great-uncle figured he'd better set Remi down and build them both a shelter.

"He lay that pup in the cranny of a rock, just in case a scavenger flew over while he was collecting branches. He lay that dog down there and he cried. He cried and cried, that old man did, thinking his dog was gone from him and nothing he could do. But it's strange how these things happen. Very strange. For your great-uncle Meyers had set old Remi in the shade beneath a big slab of stone, and from that stone, water trickled. And Remi lay there, his tongue hung out of his mouth to the side, and Meyers thought he was gone for sure. But the water that ran down from that slab trickled right onto Remi's tongue.

And sure as you sit here, that dog did wake. He woke up slowly—just one eye opened—and he looked at your great-uncle. And he whined a bit, but, little chick, he did not move. That poor old dog had lost a lot of blood. When your great-uncle looked up to thank the heavens that his old dog was still with him, there was a great big face peering out of the mountainside. Of course, this face was made of rock and it was the Wise Woman herself, looking down on the scene and taking pity on the woeful pair."

I try to look at Dawn through the shadows to see if she is hearing what Gramma just said about the Wise Woman granting a genuine miracle. But the way Dawn is sitting, her face is mostly turned in the other direction, and she doesn't glance over at me or shrug or anything. Still, she looks awake, so she must be listening.

"Your great-uncle Meyers and Remington stayed there with the Wise Woman for three days while your uncle nursed that old hound back to life. And believe it or not, your great-uncle and that hound walked out of those woods together. Remi lived five more years, making him twenty-four years old at his passing. Now, tell me that isn't a miracle right there."

Gramma clucks her tongue and is silent for a minute. And though my toes are cramping and my knee is getting a fitful bruise, I feel content and sure now of my task.

"And that is the story of your great-uncle Meyers, old Remington, and the Wise Woman of the Mountains. And you, little chick, are fast asleep. Works every time," Gramma whispers.

The lump in the back of the couch disappears, and I hear Gramma's footsteps creak away up the stairs. I let my legs unwind and rest against the back of the sofa. Pain shoots up from my feet to my knees, and I try to rub it out. A minute later, Gramma's back down the stairs. There is a click and the light that was leaking around the sides of the couch disappears. I shiver as the shadows curl around my arms. Gramma's footsteps lead away to the guest bedroom.

My eyelids feel like they have pebbles resting on them, and when I glance over at Dawn, she has shifted toward me and she looks as though she has seen a ghost. She frowns hard as she unwinds her legs.

I stand up and feel like a newborn deer, awkward on my feet. I grab Paddington, and Dawn and I step around the other side of the couch. I lean against the arm. Dawn looks at me. She turns and looks at my backpack. She peers over my shoulder and out the window to the moonlit yard.

"Maple."

"Yeah?" I whisper.

"Oh my gosh. Girls!" My heart jumps like a rabbit

scurrying from a fox. Gramma is standing at the end of the hallway with her water glass in her hand.

"What are you kids doing out of—it's nearly four o'clock in the morning!" She looks me up and down and I feel my cheeks get red. "Maple, why are you all dressed up?"

I slide the catamount paw off my head and hold both the hat and Paddington behind my back.

"Up. Up. Upstairs!" Her words are sharp. "You can tell me all about it in the morning. We need to get some sleep in this house. Let's go."

Dawn and I push up the stairs with our heads bowed low, Gramma behind us every step of the way. I kick off my shoes and Gramma helps me out of my jacket. She stares at the compass hanging around my neck and rolls her eyes. I take it off and put it next to my bed. She drops the jacket onto my chair, and I climb into my bed and try to think of excuses.

"We'll talk about this tomorrow when I have had a little bit more rest, okay?"

"Yes, Gramma," I say. She closes the door with a thump, and Curious crawls up on my bed and licks my hand.

"We didn't make it, boy, not this time around." I sink into my sheets and lay my head on Paddington's soft nose. A coyote howls in the distance. But I am inside, warm. Comfortable. Safe. And somehow that doesn't sit right with me. I turn to one side and nestle farther into my blankets. Then I switch again to the other side. I punch my pillow, lay my head down, and try to sleep.

Chapter Five

I count to two hundred twice and then start thinking on happy stuff like rainbows and sunny days, but just like that, I start thinking about Lily again, wondering if she is going to be able to have those kinds of memories to think on when she can't get to sleep. I flip over and stare at the clock. 4:15. The sky is still dark, but the moon lights the silver slivers of frost around the edges of my window.

I am about to sit up in bed when I hear a light *tap-taptap* from the other side of the room. For a minute, I dive down into my sheets, thinking it's another spooky nighttime butterfly beating away at my window when

it's supposed to be sound asleep somewhere, but then
it comes again and I can hear that it's coming from my
door. I sneak out of bed and tiptoe across the carpet.
Curious is at my heels and he is nosing around on the
floor. I open the door a tiny crack and put my eye up
close to it so I can see into the dark hallway. I can't see
Dawn real well, but I can hear her whistley breath, so I
know it's her. I guess she has come to apologize for stop-
ping my trip and ruining everything.

"What do you want?" I whisper.

"Can you let me in?" she whispers back.

"Why should I?" I say.

I hear a crinkling noise and squint my eyes to see
what she has got. I see the outline of a rolled-up map
tucked under her arm and a book and notepad in her
hands.

"What are you doing? Is that my map?" I push the
door open and she walks straight in. Curious shoots out
into the hallway.

"Maple, what I was about to tell you was, well—" I go
over to my bed and sit on the edge waiting for her to spit
it out. "I just—I didn't believe the story until Gramma
told about Remington. I'm sorry. I want to help."

I jump straight off my bed. I can't believe she is plan-
ning to come along. I give Dawn a big hug. We'll get a
miracle before tomorrow after all. I swing around to the

door and close it very gently so we don't wake Beetle up again. As I turn around I see that Dawn has pulled the thinking cap box out from under my bed and has put her top hat on. I go over to the bed and grab my catamount paw out from under my pillow where I stashed it after Gramma left. I tug it on and pull the strap down under my chin.

"So," Dawn whispers as she lays out the map of Mooreland. "What route were you going to take?" She drops a Mini Maglite out from her sleeve and clicks it on.

"I was going to figure it out when I got outside and had a chance to look at the map," I say.

Dawn laughs. "Boy, am I glad I caught you. You'd have been lost before sunup."

"No I wouldn't. Papa showed me how to use a compass and I know the directions of a map," I tell her. "I know I would have figured it out." Plus, I asked her for help earlier in the day and she wouldn't help me. It wasn't my fault I was on my way with no plan. It was hers.

"Do you even know where the Wise Woman of the Mountains stands?"

"No, well, I know she's in Vermont," I tell her. "I was going to check as soon as I got the book and then figure it out on the map. I didn't have any other choice, if you remember." I say the last part jutting my chin out toward her so she might get the hint, but she doesn't. Instead, she picks up the book she brought in. The flashlight beam rests on the title, *Mountain Legends*. She must have gotten into my backpack and helped herself to all my supplies. I cross my arms as she scans her finger down the index. She flips a few pages and scans the print. I try to get around to see what she is reading, but she won't let me have a look. She hits me with a bony elbow.

"Ouch." I push her arm, but she ignores me.

"Aha," she whispers.

"What?" I nudge in for a look. She pushes me to the side again.

"God, get off. Listen. 'The Wise Woman has been in Peninsula State Park for as long as geological explorers can explain.'"

Peninsula State Park. I have heard of it. I even think I went there on a field trip last year in Mrs. Yetti's class. I pull up to the map and just as Dawn shines her light on it, I see the name.

"Here's Peninsula State Park," I say, and lay my finger on it. Dawn rolls her eyes and flicks my hand off the map as though it were a fly on a sandwich.

"We need to find where we are in *relation* to it. It doesn't help just to know where it is," she says.

I search the lines of the map, wandering around mountain ridges and valleys, but as soon as I feel like I am getting close, the Maglite flickers and goes out.

"Stupid flashlight," Dawn whispers and slaps it against

her palm. I pull the map over to the pool of moonlight and keep looking. While Dawn is fussing with her flashlight, my eyes settle on the name of our road: Canton Creek Turnpike. I put a fingertip on it again and wait for Dawn to wave it away, but she doesn't. Instead she comes closer and looks at the map. She places the flashlight against the scale as though it were a ruler.

"One inch equals two miles," she says. Then she picks up the flashlight and places one end on Canton Creek Turnpike and one end toward Peninsula State Park. We have to move the flashlight a couple of times to get the whole distance. She sighs and drops the flashlight.

"It's nearly thirty miles from here. You never would have made it. In fact, *we're* never going to make it."

I can't believe she's saying this. I can't stand it. "We can take Millament," I whisper. If both Dawn and I rode on him, we wouldn't have to get our feet so tired, and he's big and great for hauling things. He would hardly feel us on his back.

"He's too slow, Dummy. It would take us days to get there," Dawn says.

I hate the name Dummy. Dawn is always calling me it. She thinks she is the smartest and she can do anything, but sometimes she could at least listen to some of my ideas. I start thinking on all the times she tries outdoing me. If Beetle is crying, Dawn is the one to take care of her. If I am not sure about one of my math problems from school, there is Dawn, yapping over my shoulder. If I am doing something outside, like catching myself a frog or salamander, Dawn is there telling me how I might catch one easier. I have to be quieter, or I have to reach my hand around where the frog can't see me. Those are barely any examples at all. There are a million of them. It was my idea to save the baby in the first place, and now she is taking over and being the boss.

"You really should have thought this through better," Dawn says. "We'll have to start from square one." She picks up the notepad and pulls a pencil from the top of it. And as soon as I see it come out in front of her, I knock it straight out of her hand. It rolls on the floor, pages flapping and bending. I wish part of it had ripped. I think I should have taken it and ripped it straight in half. See how many brilliant ideas she would write down then. She stretches her arm out and picks it up.

"Don't do that ever again!" she hisses and I know she is fixing to punch me one. Even in the moonlight her cheeks are getting all red.

"Don't call me Dummy ever again," I whisper, trying to keep my voice down. I stand up so I am taller than her for a minute, but then she stands up too, and she pokes that pencil into my chest.

"Maple, I am trying to help you and if all you can do is be rude to me, then you can forget it!" I feel the *bomp bomp bomp* of the eraser through my T-shirt.

"You had better stop poking me with that stupid pencil," I whisper as loud as I can.

She pinches her lips together in a look that says *Make me*. So I do. I smack that stupid pencil right out of her hand. It lands on the map and before I know it we're into it. But we have never had a middle of the night fight. It's silent and mean, no yelling, no crying. I pinch my lips shut and take the blows. I give them back too. My arms are swinging and her fists are thunking me all around. Her fingernails scrape my arms and legs. We're standing and then we aren't. We roll. One minute I hit my head against the corner of the mattress and the next minute I have the hard wood of the bookshelf jabbing into my shoulder. We roll into the moonlight, into the darkness near the door and then back again. I am huffing and puffing, trying to put up a good fight when I hear a real bad sound.

Kwiiissshhhtt.

Dawn and I both freeze. First, I think maybe it's Gramma or Beetle waking up again. I think that maybe this time the game's up. We break apart, panting heavy. I search the doorway, but it's still closed tight.

"Oh no," Dawn whispers, and I spin her way. She is staring at the map and I can see the problem right off. The pencil is lodged straight through the map and is standing on its point. A long line cuts the center.

"We're dead meat. Papa is going to kill us," I say. But Dawn's examining the map real close. She has her nose right up to it, and she is pushing the tip of her finger along the rip. She slowly moves the pencil and closes the slit, looking at it as it should be: whole.

"The river," she says real quiet at first. Quiet like hummingbird wings. You don't hear it till it has already slipped past you.

"What?" I whisper back.

Dawn holds the tear closed with one hand and traces the rip. It runs straight along a blue splash that wiggles its way down the map.

"We'll take the river. It runs directly into Peninsula State Park. We'll take the river partway and walk the last section. Why didn't I think of it before? Papa and I have gone canoeing down that way. It must be just past the Tooleys' house."

"Yes, the river," I whisper. "We'll take the river."

Chapter Six

The sun is coming up over the horizon as Dawn and I and Curious cross the porch and step down the stairs.

"I told you to leave him inside," Dawn whispers.

"You know as well as I do that he would be barking like mad if he saw us out here by ourselves," I say.

"Fine, whatever." Dawn rolls her eyes at me as we cut across the grass. I just smile, knowing she can't make me leave him now. It was scary enough opening that front door once without getting caught.

The shed creaks open and the frost on the door glitters as it swings out into the early-morning light. Those sparkles remind me of the Wise Woman and her healing powers. They make me feel warm and sure inside.

Dawn pulls the first-aid kit off the wall and shoves it into my hands. I swing the pack off my back and push the kit inside. Then we both look over at the canoe.

"You grab that end," Dawn whispers. She goes over to the other side and grabs onto it. I put my hands at the base of a rope and lift the canoe with all my strength. It barely gets an inch off the ground before Dawn is pushing it over on top of me. I fall backward and I hear the map crinkle and crunch as I land hard on the backpack.

"Maple, you actually have to lift it and walk at the same time. You can't just stand there. You think it's going to float over to the river on its own?" she says.

I want to tell her to shut her yap, but instead I get up and lift that darned thing plenty off the ground, and I move backward like I have been doing this for a hundred years. She thinks she is the best at moving a canoe, but she isn't. I can be just as good. The grass crunches under my feet as I step along to the river. It's all frosty and the ice is melting on my shoes and I can feel my feet getting a little cold and wet. We set the canoe down at the edge of the river.

"All right, I'll grab the life jackets," Dawn says and heads back toward the shed. Just then, Millament walks out of the barn and right up to the fence. The minute

Curious sees him, he wants to greet the day. He puts his nose straight into the air and starts howling. I tackle that mutt down and put my hand around his muzzle. But then Millament starts swinging his head from side to side, making as much fuss as an ox can make, mooing and clanking the bell on his neck.

"Shhhhhhhh!" I hiss at him, but he hasn't got a clue.

Curious squirms in my arms, and I crane my neck and look over at the house. The worst possible thing happens. A light flicks on. I can see the lamp in the guest room window. I send out an RSDS. An RSDS is a Rittle Sister Distress Sign and comes in the form of a birdsong. I am real good at imitating the *Poecile atricapillus*, the black-capped chickadee. *"Feebee, feebee."* As soon as I sing out the song, Dawn's head comes around the corner of the shed.

"What?" she hisses.

I point toward the house and see that Gramma has left the guest bedroom. Right then, I see her walking across the living room. She yawns for a minute and stretches. Then she looks straight out on the yard. I look at her and she looks at me. She scowls and wipes her eyes like she's not believing what she is seeing. Then it's almost as though a lightbulb switches on in her head. Her eyes pop wide and she starts moving for that door.

"Hurry!" I scream and Dawn is barreling toward me like a freight train. She is coming full throttle. She throws a life jacket at me and in the same motion throws the paddles in the bottom of the canoe. I drop Curious and he starts barking like crazy. Dawn and I push that canoe down the bank. I hear the bottom slide onto the rocks as it glides into the water.

"Go, go, go!" Dawn yells.

I jump like a bullfrog. I miss my seat, but land dead center and nearly hit my chin on the side of the canoe.

"Maple Tessa Rittle!" Gramma screams.

Gramma runs down the steps as Dawn digs into the bank with her legs. Curious barks at Gramma and then turns and makes a flying leap into the boat. He lands and his paws and nails scrape right into my jacket. The boat tips from side to side. I push him off and pull up onto my seat. Dawn jumps in and lands perfectly, ready to paddle. She pushes off just as Gramma is getting to the bank.

"Girls, girls, what do you think you are doing? Stop that boat this second!" Gramma reaches out to us, but the current is fast, and we pull away without even trying.

Gramma is barefoot in the frosty grass. She isn't wearing a jacket either and by the look she is making I wouldn't want to stop the boat if I could.

"We'll be back in a few hours, Gramma," I shout.

I try and give her reassuring looks as we speed away. But Gramma turns and runs straight for the house.

Chapter Seven

I don't ever remember being as scared as I am right now, bouncing up and down over these waves. I don't recall there being waves in the river either. At least they're not as bad when Papa steers the canoe. But here we are bouncing high and dropping low. I'm in the canoe all wrong, facing Dawn, and I'm grateful I can't see the waves splashing downriver.

Both Dawn and I have a hand on Curious's collar. One paddle is sticking up against my backpack—which keeps jumping like it is fixing to go for a swim—and the other one is in the crook of Dawn's arm.

We bounce like kids on a seesaw. My stomach is in

my shoes and then in my throat. Shoes. Throat. Shoes. Throat.

"Just one more big one! Hang on!" Dawn yells and she drops the paddle to hold on to Curious. It teeters on the side of the canoe, then the rapids swallow it and spit it out downstream. Dawn scrunches her eyes closed.

We jolt up. I hear a crunching sound, and I am off my seat. I don't want to admit it, but I yelp like a baby coyote in traffic. Dawn and Curious are sliding backward and I am toppling forward trying not to slide down the canoe. Curious's nails shriek against the wood. Next thing I know, my butt is back on the seat and over, and I land hard in the other end. Dawn and Curious topple toward me.

A second later, it all stops. The boat lands steady with some water floating in the bottom, sogging up my backpack, backside, and feet. It's the most frigid water I've ever felt and the sun is barely peeking over the horizon. Dawn picks herself up and is shaking, and I am shaking too as I pull myself up onto my seat.

"My God!" A voice breaks over the sound of the running river and right away I know it's Mr. Tooley's voice. I swivel around and catch sight of him near his truck. The hood is up and he has grease straight up to his elbows. I should have guessed he'd be out working on something. It's always work for Mr. Tooley. Day and night he is chopping wood, plowing roads, fixing up cars. From sunrise to sunset, Mr. Tooley is the busiest old man I know. When we go canoeing with Papa, we have to dock here. Mr. Tooley always shows Papa something new he crafted, or a fence he patched up, or a row he planted, and Mrs. Tooley always gives us cookies. But right now, I don't want cookies and I sure don't want to dock this boat. I smooth my hair out and put my sopping-wet hat back onto my head. The icy water drips down my face and basically freezes my thoughts.

"Hello, Mr. Tooley," Dawn says and waves like it's totally normal that we are cruising down the river alone at top speed.

But it seems like a good idea to be nonchalant, so I pitch in: "It's a wonderful day for a boat ride. Isn't it, Mr. Tooley? I am sure you would agree, and I am sure my father will agree when we meet him just two miles down at the park. He said he would meet us there, you know." After that, I set a grin with lots of teeth and gums, as wide as a big old slice of watermelon, but not as seedy.

"Hang on, kids, I'll get you, don't worry," Mr. Tooley says as he picks a branch up from the bank.

"Maybe we had better paddle," I say to Dawn. And even though I am shivering and thinking it would be nice to go inside and get some hot chocolate or sit by a warm fire, I am happy when I see Mr. Tooley miss the

edge of the boat. The branch lands in the current and we
move away from him.

"Wait, kids, back paddle," Mr. Tooley says. "Grab the
branch." He tries to reach it out to us but slips and falls
backward onto the bank.

"Go!" I whisper and Dawn grabs our last paddle
from the bottom of the boat and starts pumping.

I see Mr. Tooley jump up. "Girls, you have to stop!"
he shouts and runs alongside. "You have to get out here!
You're headed straight for the Devil's Washbowl."

Mr. Tooley crashes through the woods, but his legs
can't keep up with the current and we outrun him.

"You're headed straight for the Devil's Washbowl!
Listen to me, please!"

Dawn stops paddling and her eyes go big. But we're
too far into the current. Dawn swivels around to look at
him. But Mr. Tooley is running back toward the house.

"Harriet, Harriet, get up! Call the park ranger!" Mr.
Tooley hollers. "The Rittles are going downriver!"

We sail around a bend and the water becomes calm
and smooth, but that doesn't take the edge off how I am
all of a sudden feeling: cold and shivering and nervous
as ever.

We glide in among tall rocks, like we're at the bottom
of a gorge. The day gets darker, even though, by now, it's
supposed to be brightening and warming. Shadows wrap

themselves around us. The water appears to be black. I clamp my knees together and make sure nothing is hanging over the sides of the canoe. I scan for crocodiles even though I know that they don't live in Vermont. Dawn dips the paddle in and out of the water. When it goes in, it's barely enough to break the surface, like she is afraid it will be pulled out of her hand.

"Dawn?" I say.

"Yeah?" She pulls the paddle out of the water and sets it inside the canoe.

"What was Mr. Tooley talking about? What's the Devil's Washbowl?" I ask.

"I was going to ask you the same thing. It sounds familiar, doesn't it?" Dawn says.

It does sound familiar and I am starting to think I remember what it is, but we've never been past the Tooleys', so I am having a hard time picturing it.

Dawn tugs open my backpack and pulls out the map and the copy of *Mountain Legends*. She flips to the marked page. Her eyes zip back and forth as she searches.

Curious puts his nose in the air. His gaze darts along the ridge to the side of us. I look up to see what he sees, but it's shadowy and dark, and I don't see anything or anyone that would make him jumpy. He lifts his ears and his mouth becomes an O as he howls into the sky.

"What's there, Curious?" I say, grabbing at his collar.

"What is it?" He goes wild, howling. He points with his nose, but every time I look, I see nothing. Nothing but twiggy trees, and roots hanging over, nothing but wet moss and sharp rock that is too sheer to climb. I scan the rock face and the black water, knowing that we couldn't get out if we wanted to.

"Oh God," Dawn says, and when I look over I can tell she has found something—knows something she'd rather not know.

I lick my lips. "What? What is it, Dawn?" I ask, though I don't want to hear the answer.

"The Devil's Washbowl can be found running through Peninsula State Park," Dawn reads as she holds the book out in front of her. "It is revered by many adventurous kayakers and canoers of the highest caliber. But beware the expert and beginner alike; after a good rainfall it can sweep up into a whirlwind of rapids." She looks at me, eyes wide, then continues. "It is unpredictable to say the least. The name the Devil's Washbowl was given by Herman P. Quincy, a man who used to challenge the rapid every day in order to visit friends down the river. 'I never met a stronger or more unpredictable rapid,' said Quincy." She pauses and flips the page quickly. "'The rocks appear out of it like Satan's fingers, trying to snatch you up and throw you over. That's why I call it the Devil's Washbowl.'"

My mouth goes dry.

"You mean to say that we are headed for a heavy rapid?" I ask her.

"That is what I mean to say." She unfolds the map and points. "We're here."

I lean over Curious to see the map better. The shadows are heavy and the thin line of the river seems faded.

"And the Devil's Washbowl is"—she squints hard, moving her hand down an inch or two—"here."

I sit back up. *Think, Maple. Time to think.*

"So," I say, trying to put my words together. "So, say, say the Devil's Washbowl is coming up on us in a couple miles or so. Say these rock walls run a couple miles or so. Say they are all steep and sheer like the ones around us. How, how can we possibly a-avoid it?"

"I don't know," Dawn says. "I-I don't know if we can."

I don't know if we can? The black water ripples and Curious lets out a low quiet groan.

"It's okay, Curio," I say, and put my hand on his warm head. He licks my hand and I hear another groan. Bigger. The wind whips my ponytail up and snaps loose ends across my face. Not now. Please not now. But the sky lights up with a crash, a rumble, a lion's roar, and a giant cloud rolls in above us. Curious answers the call, his hair on end and his teeth bared. All I can do is look at Dawn, and she looks at me, and I grip the edges of the canoe as though it will give me strength. The water licks my fingers like dancing flames. The sky darkens. The shadows change from gray to dark blue. Dead leaves twirl in the sky and fall down from above. It's going to storm.

Chapter Eight

"Throw the rope!" Dawn screams into the wind.

We have come upon a clearing. Now, instead of sheer rocks surrounding us, there are banks and trees on both sides, but the current is flowing fast, sucking us like a vacuum toward the rocks downstream. We are moving too quickly to steer or grab ahold of anything.

"You have to throw the rope, Maple! It's under—" Dawn's voice falls to the waves. The rope. Of course, the rope. I look down. The rope is sprawled under my feet. I reach for it, but we hit a breaker and I lurch forward instead. Dawn screams and Curious howls. My heart thumps like a deerskin drum.

"Hurry!" Dawn says, and she gets into the middle of the canoe. I pull out the rope and she grabs the end of it. She loops it around and ties it back to itself, creating a lasso. The thunder rolls, and the boat rocks, and Curious nearly takes a swim. Dawn drops the rope to grab him.

"Throw it! To that tree!" Dawn screams.

We are sailing fast now, and I don't think that I am actually going to catch onto anything. But I look downriver, and it may be my imagination, but I swear in the distance I see rocks loom out of the water, pointy, dark, and mean. Lightning cracks and the water turns to flames.

I throw the rope. It lands on top of the water and jumps around like an angry bull. Rising and sinking in the waves.

"Pull it back!" Dawn screams. I look down the river again. My mouth goes dry. We're coming closer. I pull the rope in over the edge and throw it straight back out. Again it lands short, splashing into the water, but this time something happens. Our boat jams to a halt in the current and we spin end to end. I fall back onto Curious and Dawn.

"What happened?" Dawn says, and we untangle ourselves to peer over the side.

Dawn grabs the rope and begins to pull. I put one

hand in front of her right hand and the other behind it, and we pull hand over hand. We lurch upstream little by little. Soon I can see that our rope has snagged onto a rock. Grunting and pulling, we are nearly to it. I wipe my hair from my eyes and search the churning waves. The rock the rope is stuck on is small, and just as I spot it, the sand around it begins to give away.

"This is bad!" Dawn screams.

"We have to get out of this water now! Get out of the open," I say. Please hold on. Please let the rock hold, I pray to God and all the gods and goddesses from myths and legends I've ever heard of. I look at the water, look at the sky. I don't have to look into the waves to know that the rock lets go. I fall backward, into the belly of the canoe. My right hip digs into the seat, and in trying to catch myself, I grab onto the rough edge of the canoe. Splinters stab into my left palm.

The sky lights up again. Dawn and I both flinch as though that will save us from lightning bolts. The sky opens up and rain starts pouring down. We sail for a second. We're dead. We never should have taken the river. I bury my head in my hands and kneel in the bottom of the canoe. We're going to die. Today, in the Devil's Washbowl. I look up. We're bearing down on it. The rocks look sharp and angry and every crack of lightning reveals the boiling water ahead. Coming closer, growing larger. I can't speak or scream. I can't believe. Dawn sits in the middle of the canoe and we hug each other. Curious shakes and shivers between us.

"I'm sorry," I say, but the wind takes my voice, so I can't be sure it ever escapes my lips.

I wait for the crash. I wait. I imagine the boat exploding into splinters. I wait. Nothing happens. We bob and bounce, and my stomach spins. It almost feels like we're hardly moving. I blink. I pinch my arm. I look back at the looming rocks, but they recede and we bob and lurch closer to the shore. Little by little. Am I dreaming? I swing around and search through the rain. Has Mr. Tooley come to pull us to shore? No one's there. Dawn looks up. A second later, she is paddling our canoe upstream to the bank.

"It's an eddy!" she shouts.

I feel the vibration as our boat slides onto the shore.

"What happened?" I holler.

"We got caught in an eddy!" Dawn yells and raises her fists to the sky.

An eddy, I think, trying to remember what it is. I am about to ask her, but she is looking up at the sky, the rain running over the brim of her top hat and coming down in waterfalls around her face.

"Help me get the boat in the trees!" she says.

I pull the backpack to my shoulders, Dawn tucks the

paddle under her arm, and we lean over for the canoe. She pulls, I push. My arms burn, my hand pounds, but I dig my legs in, and the canoe slides across the sand. We take it straight toward the woods. I think of all the things Papa has taught us about lightning storms: Don't be the tallest thing in a field, don't be out in the open, don't be too close to water.

"It's going to be okay," I say. I say this to myself, to the trees, to Dawn, to my new baby sister. "It's going to be okay."

The rain pelts down angrily, soaks into my clothes and digs at my skin. Curious whines and trembles, but stays close to my leg.

We slide into the trees, the canoe moving nicely on the pine needles. The rain is less intense here, and the drops land hollowly on the forest floor.

"Just flip this up against the tree," Dawn says. Dawn and I each grab an end and flip. My arms feel heavy, like tree limbs covered in snow, but we manage to prop the canoe up on its side, leaning into a tall pine. It'll give us some shelter.

"Get in," Dawn says. I crawl into the shadows next to Curious, and Dawn crawls in next to me. We huddle together. We don't speak.

Curious curls up at our feet. I nestle my toes in under his belly. And Dawn and I hang on to each other like we're all we've got. A crack of thunder bursts, or a flash of lightning brightens the inside of our canoe with too much light, and I pray I don't get stabbed down by a lightning bolt.

I scan my body; my heart's kicking like a colt before a storm. My arms and eyelids are heavy. I feel so exhausted and so alert and scared all at the same time. All of a sudden I am thinking this isn't going to be as easy as I expected. My mind goes wild imagining. What if something comes barreling into our shelter? What if the lightning strikes us? What if the water rises and we drift away downriver?

I jump as the lightning flashes and a fluttering shadow flickers in the brief light. I freeze, searching the shadows to make out the critter. When the lightning flashes again, I see a set of beautiful brown wings perched on the inside of the canoe. *Danaus plexippus.* Just a monarch butterfly escaping from the storm. I don't know why this butterfly is haunting me, but it keeps coming around. I look at it for a minute. It's shivering, and so am I. I remember that Papa told me that they shiver to warm up so that they can fly again. Maybe it's the same for us. And I hope that it works so that we can carry on our adventure. I watch that butterfly for a long time and maybe it's the lack of sleep, or the tossing and turning in the river, or the strength it took to get around all morning, but either way, my eyes start drooping as I listen to the thrumming of that rain. Even though I am shivering and cold, I curl up with Dawn and Curious and fall straight to sleep.

Chapter Nine

Birds twitter in the treetops. I peel my eyes open. Where am I? What happened? My eyes slowly focus and I see the inside of the old canoe peering down at me. The baby, Gramma, Mr. Tooley, and the rainstorm tumble through my mind. I jerk to a sitting position, nearly colliding with the wood above. My head reels and I fall back down to my side. My whole body aches.

I push myself over Dawn, along the forest floor and out into the sun. I lean up against the other side of the pine tree and examine my hand. Seven splinters are deep under my skin. It looks red and shiny as though it is getting infected. I close my fingers and lean my head against the tree.

The air is still cold and I shiver again without Dawn next to me. My jacket's wet, and my pants are stiff with water and cold. Curious comes through the trees, and his feet disappear in red and orange leaves and dried brown pine needles. He pauses and sniffs the ground. The trees are separated here and it looks like he is in the divot of an old logging road. He sniffs and laps some water from a puddle that has formed in it. Then he looks up and trots over to me, his mouth wide with a smile.

"You happy in the woods, boysie?" I ask as he comes over and lies down by my side.

"This is awful," Dawn says as she pulls herself out from under the canoe. "I feel like I've been hit by a train." She rubs her hand across her face. Pine needles fall down her side as she wobbles to her feet.

"I feel the same way," I say, "but at least we're alive."

"No kidding." She walks over to me slowly, rubbing her arms with her palms. "I'm freezing," she says.

"Me too. Do you think we have time to build a fire?"

"I don't think we have any other choice, Maple. I'm not going to be able to walk far if I am shivering the whole time. Shivering takes up an enormous amount of energy. I say we build a fire and try to get our heads back on straight. I'll get some kindling wood. Did you bring matches?"

"Yeah," I say as she walks a distance into the trees.

I pull the backpack out and dig in up to my elbow. Everything is sopping wet. I lay some of my clothes out on the forest floor and hang others off tree branches. I pick up *Mountain Legends*. The pages are wrinkling, so I open it and lean it against a tree. I slowly unroll the map. It's wet and threatening to rip straight in half, but I manage to lay it down without ruining it.

I open the front zipper of my backpack and pull out the Ziploc bag, my emergency fire-starting kit. My matches kept good and dry. This is a trick Papa showed me. Always keep matches and some lint from the dryer inside a plastic bag and fire is one match strike away. Dawn drops some twigs next to me and then goes back to get some more wood.

I take the lint out of the Ziploc and pile a few twigs around it. I pile some dried, dead pine needles along with them. The pine needles don't take long to burn, but they will help if everything else is wet. Dawn comes back with a few bigger pieces and starts breaking them so they are about the length from my fingers to my shoulder. I set them up against each other, make a teepee.

"I found some dead branches. It was hit or miss, but these few are dry. It will be a good start until we get it burning," Dawn says as she picks up the Ziploc and takes out the box of matches. She strikes one and sneaks it into the teepee, straight to the ball of lint. The lint lights and sparks, and I blow on it gently from the other side. The pine needles pop, and smoke billows up. I close my eyes and keep blowing into the fire.

"It's almost there," Dawn says, and she gets on the other side and we take turns stoking it. Between the two of us the twigs burn and the fire begins to eat away at the bigger branches. It's real smoky, but at least it's something. My face feels like it is thawing out as I lean nice and close. If we can just get warmed up, soon the sun will be pouring down and we will be plenty warm and dry for the journey. I sit back on my heels.

"Maple. We need to go home. I—this isn't going to work. We almost got killed trying to get here," Dawn says as she puts a few more twigs into the fire.

Her words are like a slap in the face. Why go to all this trouble and turn around? I'm too tired for this right now. My head pounds and I close my eyes to trap the tears.

Dawn continues, "Maybe we should make signals with the smoke."

As tight as I am closing my eyes, tears still escape and slip down my cheeks.

"No," I say, wiping my face. "I have to keep going."

"We can't. We don't even know if this is going to work. We—"

"Stop, Dawn," I say. "I'm aching and sore too. But the baby needs a miracle. She's not doing well. Dad said so on the phone. You heard him. We can't give up. I believe in the Wise Woman. If she could cure Remi, then she can cure our sister. C'mon. We're halfway there."

Dawn's shoulders come down and her head drops. "I don't like this idea. I'm your big sister, and I am supposed to keep you safe, and I am telling you, this is not a good idea. Mama and Papa would not like this."

"Well," I say, "you might be my big sister, but I'm a big sister too. I have to do something. I have to keep going. If you want to go with the park ranger when he comes, then go ahead. But I am not leaving without that water."

Dawn's sigh sounds more like a growl, and her eyes flash at me. "I am not about to let you go on alone. You'd get lost, hurt, maybe even killed."

"Yeah, but if we get the water and get back safe, we can cure the baby," I say, my face covered in tears now. "This is her chance, Dawn."

Dawn is silent for a minute. We both sit close to the fire. I watch the sun come through the trees' pointy bare branches. I rub my arms and legs, try to get the blood flowing in them.

"Did you bring a mirror or anything for us to signal with?" Dawn says.

She is not even listening to me. Now she is looking up into the sky for airplanes.

"I told you, I am not going to go back without the water," I say.

"This isn't safe," she says.

I want to tell her she doesn't know everything. She thinks she is the smartest person in the world, but she's not. I want to tell her that she can't talk to me like this anymore. I'm old enough to make my own decisions. But instead of talking, my muscles get tight, and I stand up and grab her top hat out from under the canoe. She rolls her eyes at me.

"You think you're so smart, and you never listen to anything I say! It's like the only thing that matters is the stuff that *you* think matters!" I shout.

The fabric of the old top hat is still wet from the rain, but I clamp it between my fingers and thumb and I lift my kicking leg as high as I can and smack the top straight off that top hat. It rips easily and my leg goes through up to my knee. I pull it off my leg and toss it on the ground.

She tackles me before I can take a breath. Then we're in the pine needles and rolling. My cap flies off my head, and she scrambles after it across the forest floor. But I grab both her legs and punch her hard in the calf. She doesn't even seem to feel it. Then she tries thumping me in the face but I block her with both my hands and I push her with my legs. She falls backward, but her sharp fingers dig into my leg. My skin crumples and it feels like I have an angry snapping turtle stuck on my shin. I scream and kick at her and she lets go and nearly rolls into the fire, but stops just next to it, panting.

I lay still. The pine needles dig into my back. My head buzzes. I lie on the ground and rub my leg. Curious grips my hat between his teeth and brings it over to me.

"Thanks, boysie," I say, patting him on the chin. "I knew we should have come alone." I look over at Dawn to make sure she hears me, but now she is holding her top hat in her hands and peering down at it as though she has got a wounded animal or something. She turns it around over and over again like she is trying to figure out how to breathe strength back into it.

"I can't believe you," she says and just like that she's crying right into her hat. Something twists and snaps inside of me like a little tree branch in a storm.

"Grampa gave me this!" She smacks me in the arm and walks away from me, twisting the cap between her fingers.

I remember now that she got that from Grampa Jakes. That he said if she wanted to be the smartest in her class, then she should wear it while she was studying. I try and stomp out the feeling in the pit of my stomach, but I can't. Here I am trying to save one sister while hurting the other. I try and think of what Mama or Papa might say.

"Dawn!" My voice comes out sharp and gravelly. "We need to work together!" She stops mid-step and turns toward me.

"Maple." She pauses. "You don't get it. I'm trying to keep you out of trouble—"

"Well, that's great, but I'm not the one in trouble here, Dawn. I am trying to fix things, so let's stop trying to keep me out of trouble and try to get our little sister out of trouble!" My voice rises the whole time until I am practically screaming.

She doesn't say anything, but she doesn't leave either. She doesn't come back and fight me. She sits down and I sit down and we don't talk for a while. I pull off my shoes and leave them wide open next to the fire. I fan out the bottoms of my pants and I take off my jacket and hang it on a tree limb. It will take the longest to dry. I start making a plan, scrambling around in my head trying to figure out how to convince her to see my side.

I don't get real far before she says, "Mr. Tooley said he was calling the park ranger. We'll go as far as we can before we run into him. One person will carry the bag, and the other will carry the compass and lead, then we'll switch. I'll lead first."

She peels off her shoes and places them by the fire. Then she pulls off her jacket and hangs it next to mine.

I pull the map over to me. I follow the rip down, locate the Devil's Washbowl, and put my finger on it. I search the valleys and mountains. I find the Wise Woman, and I put my finger on that too.

"It's a ways north," Dawn says, and I see she is leaning in to see also. She puts her index finger and thumb up to the scale and then measures the distance between my fingers. "Yes, about ten miles. Let's throw some more wood on this fire." I put a few new branches on it, and stretch my toes to the warmth. Dawn may not be with me. But she isn't against me. The most I can hope for is fast travel and no pesky rangers.

Chapter Ten

"This way," Dawn says as we cut through the trees. She does this every so often, I guess to remind me that she is leading, that she knows where she's going. I grit my teeth and follow behind her. The backpack is digging into my shoulders, and every once in a while I check on my palm. It's getting itchy now. I scrape at it with my fingernails, and think about putting some first-aid cream on it, but we wasted enough time already.

Our clothes dried pretty quick, but the jackets stayed wet. I crammed mine back into the backpack, and Dawn is wearing hers around her waist. It's starting to warm up a little bit, so our sweatshirts are okay. I have the hood up around my head to keep my ears from feeling the chill.

The sun is streaming and the day is turning out pretty nice. There is a little crisp fall feeling to the air. It's mostly cold in the shadows. We try to avoid them, walking in the sunny spots. I aim for one, and when I get to it, I pick a new one to aim for. When I tire of that, I start thinking on Beetle, wondering what she's been up to, then I start thinking on Lily, and I hope she can see the sun from her room at the hospital. I hope she can smell the autumn leaves.

We come along a big sunny patch, and I start whistling. Dawn turns around and tells me to knock it off, so I whistle a little bit more. There's no reason I can't whistle when I want to.

"Quiet," Dawn says as we come through a stand of pines and into a clearing.

I whistle a little bit louder to show her that I know I'm getting under her skin.

"I said quiet!" Dawn says as she crouches down in the underbrush.

I sing out the song of the *Poecile atricapillus* and sure enough a black-capped chickadee answers me from the treetops. I spin around and sing at him again, and he echoes my call.

"Quiet! Do you hear something?" Dawn says.

"Yeah, a chickadee," I say.

Dawn grabs my arm and pulls me down next to her.

"Hey!" I say, and she pulls my backpack off my back. 'Bout time—it was her turn to carry it. But she lets out a sharp whistle between her teeth, and Curious comes in close to us.

"Grab him," she says.

"What's going on?" I say, noticing the beads of sweat on her forehead.

"Quiet," she says and glares at me. This time I plant my lips shut and perk up my ears. I hear something. A low, quiet rumble. So low, I almost feel it before hearing it.

"What is it?" I whisper.

"I don't know," she says as she pulls out the binoculars. She puts them right up to her face and lies down on her stomach. Curious starts to pull away from me.

"Stop it, boysie," I whisper at him. I feel the ground shake under me and the rumbling gets a little bit louder.

I hold Curious under my arm and look at Dawn. Her jaw drops.

"What is it?" I say as I lay down on my stomach next to her. She puts the binoculars up to my face and points.

A jeep is rolling slowly into the clearing. Park ranger. Great. I look over at her. Why isn't she running out there waving him down?

"What's going on with you?" I whisper.

"Look closer," she says. I peer out, focus in on the jeep. One driver. One passenger. The jeep crawls across the grass and turns straight for us.

Trevor Collins. Dawn's archenemy from school. I read about him a million times in her diary. I remember, now, that his father is the park ranger for Peninsula State Park. Trevor is always bragging about going out with his old man on jobs.

I shrink farther into the bushes. Dawn's face is as red as a beet. Her jaw is set in a mean line. She drops the binoculars, and I try to read what she is thinking.

Curious spots the pair of them and I can see he is about to let out a long howl. I clamp my hand around his muzzle.

"Quiet, Curio," I whisper. "Trust me."

He lies on his belly and paws at my hand.

"Weren't you saying that you wanted to stop when the ranger came?" I whisper. "You could go with them. Tell them I got lost—"

"I am not going to be rescued by Trevor Collins, not in a million years," she whispers and looks at me as though I am an albino deer. She's never seen one in her life.

The sound of the jeep grows louder and we shrink into the shadows.

"Do you see them, son?" Mr. Collins says in a low voice.

"No, sir, but we men better find them soon. They won't last long in these parts," Trevor says.

Dawn nearly spits on the ground. Her nostrils flare.

"Yes, son," Old Man Collins says.

"Just like a couple of girls to think they can take off down the river," Trevor says.

I almost drop Curious to look for a good throwing rock.

"Don't," Dawn whispers, looking at me. "You don't want to be stuck with him the whole way back to town. Trust me."

"He thinks he's so smart. I can't stand—"

"Shhh," Dawn whispers. The tires get louder, slower, and I can tell they're a few feet from us. Curious goes wild, trying to see what's out there. I press him into the dirt, but his collar still lets out a jangle as he tries to pull free.

Stop it, Curio, stop it, I think, trying to send him the message with my eyes, but a second later he yanks and his collar pulls the tender skin on my palm. I let go and grab my hand as he bounds out into the open.

"Ho there! Look, Pop!" Trevor yelps.

We're done for. I lie flat on my stomach, trying to see through the leaves. Curious is out there, proving his name. He's sniffing the tires, and as soon as they climb down, he is sniffing their hands and faces.

"You with the girls? Are ya, boy?" Trevor says to Curious. "Where are they? Where are they, boy?"

"I guess that's that," I say.

Dawn groans. "Over my dead body are we Rittle sisters going to get in the car with Trevor Collins. I'm sure he'll get a medal for rescuing us, and us not even in need of rescuing."

"But I thought that—"

"Forget what I said. Quiet. Now is not the time."

I quiet down all right, but can't help but let a little smile cross my lips.

"I'll check the perimeter, son, you see if you can get him to follow a scent. Where'd he dart out from, anyway? Was it over here?" Mr. Collins heads straight for us. His footsteps clomp and scuff through the grass and dead leaves, and I lay with my cheek straight down in the dirt. Dawn is hunched over and we both are as close to the bush as we can get without getting prickers in our sides. I can see the toe of his work boots through the leaves. Brown and covered in mud. I can almost smell them from here. I hold my breath and Dawn bites her lip.

"I think I see a couple of footpr—"

Schoo-schoo-schoo.

I don't know who sends them, but at that moment a flurry of partridge fly right out across the field. Curious goes wild after them. He howls and sets off into the trees.

"What the— Don't let him go, son. Grab him!" Mr. Collins yells. His boot spins in the grass and I watch him stomp across the field. His boots are too big for running, and he looks awkward, like an injured heifer.

"We need his help tracking!" he hollers as he disappears into the trees after his son.

Dawn's leg is pressed against mine and I can feel her laughing. I can't help myself. I start in too.

"Did you see him run?" she giggles.

"He looked like a wounded animal," I say, slapping her on the back. For a while we just sit there. My belly is aching, picturing Old Man Collins yelling at his son. But then I think on Curious.

"What if they don't get him? What if he gets lost?" I say.

"Oh, please," Dawn says. "That dog could find his way home from China if he had to, but they'll probably catch him and have him home by supper time."

"Well, if we want to meet him there, I think we had better get on with it. Are you willing to come with me?" I say.

Dawn laughs. "I'm willing to go on as far as we can without getting caught by the dreadful duo."

"It's a deal—"

"If," Dawn says, "you apologize for ripping the top out of the hat that Grampa gave me." She pauses again.

"The hat I wear all the time, that is the only thing that
I have of his."

It was pretty sour of me to do that.

"Sorry," I say. "I shouldn't have done that. I'm sure I
can patch it up when we get home."

Dawn nods. "I would appreciate that, Maple."

We both get up off the ground and look out toward
the hills. The sun has been climbing ever since we landed
by the river and it feels like we're just beginning.

"Nine miles until a miracle," I say.

"Maybe a little less," Dawn says, and we crouch along
the tree line until that jeep is long out of sight and mind.

Chapter Eleven

The journey takes us through dense woods with no path to follow, and then open fields with no footprints but our own. I wonder how long it has been since people have come this way. We passed a few old logging roads, but Dawn says those have probably been out of commission for a while now, ever since this piece of land was turned into a state park. Probably used only by Mr. Collins. I guess she's right on this, since I swear I see tire tracks running all along them.

I imagine people still come to see the Wise Woman. I know Mama said that people visit her less and less, but surely she still gets some visitors. And I keep expecting to run into fellow travelers.

We slide on pine needles and scuff through dead, decaying leaves. We switch the backpack, from Dawn to me and back again, and we each keep an ear and an eye out for the sound or sight of that park ranger jeep. I listen for Curious's collar jangling in the distance, but all I hear are birds and the occasional skitter of a squirrel or chipmunk chase.

"Maple, are you hungry?" Dawn says, and thank goodness too. I am starving.

We come to the top of one hill and it sprawls out into a good flat field. We find a spot near the wood line, just in case we have to duck into the shadows. I drop onto my knees and pull out our water bottle. I'm so thirsty and my head feels like it is filling with cotton. I take a good long chug, then I pass it to Dawn and she takes a few gulps too.

I pull out a T-shirt and wipe the sweat off my face. The material catches on my palm and it seems to sizzle and come alive as though there are little bugs moving around under my skin. It looks red and feels awful tender. Dawn looks over and I flip my hand fast. I don't want her to see the swelling . . . she'll probably tell me all about what I should be doing with it, and decide we'd better go back and get help or something dumb like that.

"Well, let's see. We have beans and kielbasa," I say.

"That's a good lunch. It'll give us energy for the remainder of the trip," Dawn says. I can't help but smile when she says "remainder of the trip."

"Perfect," I say.

I pull out my emergency meal, which is still wrapped up in my handkerchief, and hand the can of beans to Dawn. Then I start working at the handkerchief knot. I can smell the cabbage leaves before I even open the package. They are smashed together and wet. The kielbasa looks okay, though.

Dawn arches her eyebrows at me as I toss the cabbage leaves into the trees. She places the can of beans on the ground and starts prying the lid off with her Swiss Army knife. The smell of the beans wafts over, sweet and fatty, and they cover up the smell of the cabbage and make my appetite come back good and strong. I don't love baked beans cold. The way I love them best is when Gramma makes them fresh, but my mouth starts to water all the same. I didn't realize I was quite this hungry.

I pull the waxy wrapping from the meat and take a big bite out of the end of it. It tastes spicy and delicious and I feel stronger already.

Dawn grabs a camping spoon—it looks like a fork and a spoon put together—and she digs into the thick beans.

"Want some?" she asks, handing me the can. We trade and I have some beans. They cool my mouth and taste like candy compared to the sausage.

"I want to check where we are on the map," Dawn

says and she pulls it out of the backpack. The section of it that has been hanging out of the top is completely dry now. She unrolls it carefully and I put my good hand under the damp part, to make sure it doesn't split off.

Dawn checks her watch. "We have been walking for, well, including the episode with the stupid park ranger, we have been walking for about two and a half hours."

I can't believe it.

"Shouldn't we be there by now?" I ask, trying to do the math in my head.

"Maple, no, obviously. The Wise Woman is about ten miles north of the Devil's Washbowl, remember," she says and looks up at the sky. "We got caught up by that park ranger. That lost us some time. We are both sore from that canoe fiasco." She rolls her shoulder and her neck and I stretch my sore arm and open and close my hands.

"It's ascending terrain," she continues, "so of course we will be a little bit slower. With all that put together, we still probably have six or seven miles to go."

"I can't believe that," I say. I peer in closer to the map. But I hate to admit I am not sure what to look for. Dawn must see me looking confused.

"Well," Dawn says, "if we are going two miles per hour and we have been walking for about two hours, then we would be around *here*." Dawn points her finger to where we are supposedly standing. "See, this was the first field we walked through, and if I am right, this is the field we are sitting next to right now." She is pointing to a tiny green circle no bigger than my thumbprint, but it makes sense. Which means we still have a long way to go.

"Okay. Okay," I say. "We have to pick up the pace."

"Good idea," Dawn says. "Except the incline is going to increase before it decreases, and that could make us go even slower. Also, we have to factor in fatigue."

I don't want to hear any of this. I just want to get there and get back.

"Fine. Well, that means that we had better cut this break short." I look up at her but my voice lodges in my throat, and the song of the black-capped chickadee flies from my lips, because just past her blue eyes there is a set of brown ones. Wide and round and with a nose that is sniffing for beans in syrup, or maybe a kielbasa link. A black bear. Big and hungry.

Chapter Twelve

Jeez Louise. I have never been so close to a wild animal before in all my life. Well, a moose once, but never anything with such big teeth. I grab Dawn by the shoulder and we both jump to our feet as though there is a sudden grass fire. The black bear must not like the quick moves, because he bounces like he is getting ready to run. I am feeling like running myself.

"Don't run," Dawn whispers to me. I try to tell my legs to stand still, but they're popping like touch-me-not seeds. The bag, map, and compass are lying there on the ground next to that black bear's meaty paw. I want to grab them, to keep them with me so we can get to the Wise Woman. Dawn must see me eyeing our goods.

"Don't make any sudden moves. Let's, let's just back up really slowly," she barely whispers.

I try to remember some things about black bears, like if they maul humans and eat them for lunch.

"Black bears don't eat meat," I say. The black bear steps toward us, and I take a teensy step back.

"Yes they do," Dawn whispers. "Black bears are omnivorous."

Jeez Louise. This is not happening. The black bear's fur is glistening and his eyes are beady. He looks us over and his nose starts going wild, wiggling back and forth, like he is sniffing our delicious human flesh.

He inches closer and I can see he has some big claws under his fur. They are long and black and sharp. *Bears eat berries,* I say to myself, *and grass before they hibernate.* But my legs don't stop jumping. My teeth don't stop smashing into each other like they have a mind of their own. I hear Dawn's quick breath. I see the map, the contents of our bag, spilling out. I feel the breeze across my face. Then something flits out of a shadow. It seems to appear out of nowhere. The monarch. It gently flaps and flutters down. It lands its tiny body right on the compass. I am betting it's the same one we saw earlier in the day. Just like that, I remember our cause. I remember what it is we are doing. If Davy Crockett could grin down a bear, I could at least try and scare one.

I feel the catamount paw on the top of my head, and

I pull the strength down into my chest and into my legs.
I look into the bear's eyes. He inches forward. His pink
tongue lolls from his mouth, and his teeth glisten in the
sun. The birds in the trees stop twittering, the grass stops
rustling, the squirrels and chipmunks seem to stand still.
All I can hear is buzzing in my ears.

My body moves on its own. My throat lets loose a
scream and it is part wild holler and part growl. I don't
run but my legs pump in place and I stomp the ground
with my feet. I hit one foot and then the other into the
earth. Through my body and into my ears, my stomps
drum as loud as thunder.

The bear lurches sideways so quickly it looks like
he almost leaves his fur behind. It shakes loosely on his
body. His hind legs land on our map and it rips as he
twirls in the other direction. The can of beans spills, but
he snags the kielbasa before he jets out across the field.
My scream dies as the distance between us grows, and
my legs buckle under me. I can hear my breathing. I can
hear Dawn breathe. I can hear the woods wake up and
the animals sing their songs.

"He's gone," Dawn says. *"He's gone!"* she screams into
the sky. Then she starts to laugh and I start to laugh,
banshee laughs, uncontrollable and high. But as it begins,
my heart tugs, and I start crying too. I am laughing and
crying at the same time. Frantic and relieved.

"Well, there goes lunch," Dawn says, wiping her eyes.

"Yeah," I say. My stomach grumbles as I look at the torn map, smudged with beans. Papa's not going to be happy about that. My gaze floats from the map to the line of trees ahead. I look to our left and see the sun is just above us, maybe even heading toward the west.

"We'd better get going," I say, and dust the beans off the map.

"Yeah," Dawn says.

"Are you all set?" I ask her.

"Sure," she says, taking a deep breath and looking off into the distance. Then it's as though she is reading my thoughts. "At the rate he is going, he is probably a mile away by now."

"Yeah," I say, and say it again inside my head.

"Let's go." Dawn picks up the spilled can of beans. There's only a small amount left in the bottom.

I pick up the compass. The monarch is gone now. I didn't see it leave, but it's nowhere to be found. I put the compass to my waist and spin until the needle settles on the *N*. I look out to where it points. And as we walk I can't stop thinking about the baby and the butterfly and what a weird day it has been.

Chapter Thirteen

As we walk, I scrape the last of the beans out of the can, and Dawn puts it into our backpack. We hop over a mountain stream, and I push the branch of a pine tree out of my way.

"Can you believe it, Maple? *Ursus americanus*. A real live black bear. I can't believe it. I mean, this late in the fall, I assumed it would be hibernating. I wish we had had a camera—Mama and Papa won't believe this when we tell them."

She rambles on and on.

"I remember seeing all the bears at the Fairbanks Museum and the black bear was practically the smallest one there. But he was still huge. I'm still shaking. Wow. I can't wait to tell Mrs. Sykes."

Mrs. Sykes is Dawn's teacher. She loves Mrs. Sykes and is always talking about her like she is the smartest person in the world. I think she basically wants to be Mrs. Sykes when she grows up.

The trees here are dense and we are bushwhacking through them. Dawn holds a branch out and I take it so it doesn't hit me. The pine needles scrape my palm and I almost yelp, but I shut my lips tight, not wanting Dawn to know anything about it. Still, I figure I had better take a good look at it. I try and give it a sideways glance, but every second, there is Dawn turning around, telling me more about the black bear.

"Did you know that they actually have better navigational abilities than humans? They also see in color, and their noses are far more capable than the human nose."

Though I am learning a lot about black bears, my hand is starting to itch. I rub my palm.

"Hey, Dawn, I have to make a pit stop."

"Fine. I'll look out for bears."

I move away from her and head off through the trees.

"Don't go too far, Maple," Dawn says.

"I'm right here, Dawn," I say. But I move a little farther, just in case she tries to come and check on me. I walk until I can only see her backpack in the distance and then I squat out of sight. I uncurl my fingers. My

palm is red and puffy. I push on one of the splinters
and a little bit of white runs out. I wipe it off and look
around for something to put on it. If only I had that
backpack. I push at another splinter and consider dress-
ing it with mud or something.

I am looking around for mud when I hear a little
noise. I move toward it, wondering if maybe it's Curious.
I stay low in case it's not. I tread quiet as I can through
the trees. A minute later I come up right at the edge
of a field. I get down low and scoot up under a bush
to look out. Right off, I see the cause for all the noise.
Three brown deer stand before me. Deer are beautiful
and these deer look like a good solid family. There is one
that stands tall like a king, his antlers reaching toward the
sky. The doe has soft eyes and beautiful fur as though
she has been to the groomer, and the fawn is looking like
it's growing up fine. You can barely see what's left of its
baby spots. The doe puts her muzzle to the ground and
nibbles the grass.

Schwiiipt-da. A sound breaks through the trees and I
freeze. The doe and the fawn raise their tails and bust
into the woods. The buck takes a few quiet leaps and
then crumples. I stare at him. An arrow sticks out of his
side.

"It's bow season," I whisper, wiping the tears from
my eyes. It's bow season.

I want to turn and go, but Dawn's RSDS comes

through the trees: *"Thweet thweet. Thweet thweet."* The song
of *Cyanocitta cristata*, the blue jay. I tell myself not to
move. I peer around, scanning the perimeter of the field.
Then I spot her, just over to my left, hiding among the
bushes. I can barely make out her image, but I think she
puts her finger to her lips. A second later she ducks into
the shadows and I do the same, hunkering low and quiet
in my spot.

Two men walk into the field. They're dressed in
full camouflage. Their faces are painted green and black.
They have black rings around their eyes. One of them
holds a bow while the other one carries a knife. They
don't speak. They signal to one another.

Just like that, I know what's wrong. There's no hunting in Peninsula State Park. They're poachers. Whoever
is doing this is doing it illegally. I put a hand over my
mouth to muffle my breathing.

The poachers approach the deer slowly. It jerks
around and tries to stand, not completely dead, but not
really alive. Its eyes are wide and they move about franti-
cally. Saliva runs out of its mouth and across its velvet
hide.

I've never seen an animal die before. Sure, during
hunting season I've seen deer hanging upside down from
the barn door, and I've seen dead partridge getting their
feathers plucked out, and I even saw a dead raccoon

once. But the animals would be clear into heaven when I
saw them, and we didn't waste a bit of them. Papa made
me a drum out of the deer hide, and Mama and Papa
made venison jerky and venison steaks. But this buck, it
was so alive a minute ago and now it writhes in a place
in between. The man with the knife raises it over his
head.

"Oh, no," I whisper. *Quiet as a catamount*, I think to
myself. *Quiet as a catamount. Quiet, quiet, quiet.*

I try to turn away, but I can't. It's as though my head
is being held still. My eyes stuck open. The man grunts
as he forces the knife into the deer's chest. Blood spills
out over his hand and the buck shudders, flails, and finally lays still. My stomach feels so tight it could explode.
I turn away from the scene and rest my face against the
ground, focusing on nothing but breathing air in and out.
The men don't talk. But they must be moving around in
the clearing. Their shoes pound the ground and are so
loud through the earth that they sound like the footsteps
of giants.

I lie like this in the shadows for what seems like an
eternity. Finally, one of the men speaks, in a whisper. I
look up.

The man with the bow strapped to his back drags the
buck's body across the field. Its belly is wide open now,
his insides left somewhere for birds and rodents. A red

trail runs behind it, made of flattened grass and pools of blood. The men are almost to the trees. Almost gone and leaving us room to sneak away, to continue our journey, but just as they reach the corner of the field I hear Dawn throw up somewhere in the shadows. The men stop.

Chapter Fourteen

They move like predators, one on each side of the clearing, closing in. My heart hammers the ground, and I imagine Dawn's is doing the same. Two important things are flashing through my mind. One is that they think that Dawn is really an animal and they are going to dive in to kill when they reach her. Second, if they reach her and find out she is a girl and not an animal, then she is going to get in bad trouble anyway. See, poachers don't like to get caught. I know this for a fact 'cause Papa's friends with Mr. Dogwood, the game warden, and Mr. Dogwood got beaten up bad trying to stop poachers one night. My stomach flips as they walk toward her. The man closest to me steps past my hiding place. And I pretend I am frozen stock-still. He wipes his knife on his sleeve but keeps it gripped in his hand. He makes a signal to the other man—he shrugs his shoulders and points toward Dawn's hiding place. I don't see her. I wonder if she has scooted back. The other man hunches his shoulders, palms facing the sky. But they keep moving toward her. They keep going toward my sister. I scramble for a plan. I think ten things at once. Should I run and jump onto one of their backs? Should I throw a rock and see if I can knock one out? Should I holler for Dawn to run? They move closer and I haven't got any good ideas.

I can't see Dawn, but all I can picture is her sitting past the wood line, hiding up against a tree, about to get stabbed. I shuffle around looking for a stick, or a rock, but there is nothing within my reach.

The men slow down as they get closer. They signal to each other with their fingers to their lips. Be quiet, they say. Sneak up to kill. One of the men leans down and puts a hand out toward the bush, the bush I know Dawn is lying somewhere behind. His hand is about to grab the leaves. My throat tightens up and my blood seems to flood my head. There's nothing I can think to do but run. And that's it, that's what I do. I push backward away from the field and then bust like a catamount through the trees.

"Something's there! Get after it, Leroy. Get after it!"

I can hardly see where I am going, I move so fast. I am dodging trees and jumping downed logs. I hear the men crashing behind me. I use the tight trees to my advantage, jumping between limbs and running through thick brush. My sweatshirt sleeves get torn up right away, and I start feeling scrapes on my skin, but it's working. They're following.

"You see it, Leroy?" I hear one of the men shout. "What kind of critter is it?"

"I don't know. But I do see fur," another says.

My catamount paw. They think I'm an animal.

"Let's take a shot, Leroy."

My legs have a mind of their own when I hear those words. I have never moved them so fast, and it's almost like they're propelling themselves. I am just along for the ride. I look right and left through the trees. Praying that something happens. That someone shows up, that another animal barrels through. I want to hide inside a log, or in the hollow of a tree, but I swear I'm looking everywhere, and I'm not finding one.

Schwiiipt. Thunk. An arrow lands in a tree as I pass it. My heart feels like it's going to burst right out of my chest. This is the dumbest thing I've ever done. I'm thinking maybe if I holler and surrender, they wouldn't shoot a little girl. But who knows? Another arrow whizzes by my head. *Thunk.* I see a clearing up ahead. I figure if I get out of these dense trees, they'll see it's me. See it's a person, not some animal. I break through the wood line and just as I realize the clearing is a pond, the ground disappears from beneath me and I am falling. Twigs catch my arms and legs and a tree limb hits me right beneath my left eye. Then I fall into the dark and land in pool of water, dizzy and panting hard.

I hear a crash and then a splash and my heart nearly makes me deaf with its beating. But I listen.

"Where'd it go? You see it, Leroy?"

"I don't see a thing, Jim."

Then something else happens. A low hollow echoing reaches my ears: *thwap thwap*, like a sheet in the wind. Only right off I realize it can't be that. I look around and it seems like I am in an igloo made of tree limbs. It's then everything ties together. I am in a genuine beaver lodge and that thwapping, that's a beaver slapping his tail against the surface of the water. That's a warning.

"It's a beaver, Jim."

"Well, he's right there. Take aim, Leroy."

"He's ducked under."

"Shoot, you idiot. I can see the trail."

I hear an arrow hit the water and my whole body shakes.

"Weak, Leroy. You got to learn to take aim. You got to know where it's going, not just where it's been."

"It was moving fast. You wouldn'ta done any better."

The voices start to head the other way.

"Pretty sure I been doing better all day."

I sit there still until I can't hear their steps anymore. Then I put my finger up to my cheek. It's bloody for sure. So is my arm, and I have a good scrape running down my leg. I realize before long that I am whimpering and I think that's stupid, 'cause I have to be brave and still get the water for the baby, only I'm not quite sure if the poachers are gone. I am not quite sure where Dawn is. And I am not quite sure how to find her again. And I want to scream and holler out her name, but that isn't an option 'cause I don't want to get shot down.

I pick myself up and sit on my knees. And I fix my catamount paw hat, which has slipped to the side of my head. And I think to myself that if Dawn were here, she would have a real good idea on how to find her again. But I'm on my own.

Chapter Fifteen

B.O.A.P.E. is what you do in an emergency. Papa taught us this rhyme to help us remember what to do in "red flag" situations. This is one of those situations right now.

B stands for Breathe: Papa says that you can't do much in a panic and also that panicking is a big waste of energy. Step one makes you slow your body down. I take a long deep breath in and a long slow breath out to calm my soul. Besides shivering, I feel a tiny bit better, but still not anywhere near good.

O stands for Observe: Papa says you have to take in your surroundings. I look around myself. I am in a beaver lodge. It appears to be built half on the bank and half in the shallow water. I'm kneeling in pond water which is almost covering my knees. I can see a dark hole that leads into the murky water and remember what I learned in ELF—Environmental Learning for the Future or Fun or something program in Mr. Crock's class. Beaver lodges like this have an entrance that is usually underwater, so that the beaver can exit and enter from the pond. It's sort of like a secret underground tunnel. Also, they cake the whole lodge with lots of grass and mud to keep it tightly closed and warm. I look close and sure enough, there is dried mud, grass, twigs, and even pebbles and rocks built into the walls. I don't know how I managed to bust through the top, though. I look around some more and realize that the back side of the lodge is pure mud, just earth itself. This means that the lodge is built straight up against a ledge. I lucked out by running directly onto it. If I had been three feet to the right or the left, I would have simply fallen into the pond. I would have been in plain sight, probably would have been shot straight through.

I look at the hole I made in the top of the lodge and a chickadee flies across the sky above. I perk up my ears and I hear the sounds of the forest. I know for a fact that when we were running, the birds stopped chirping, probably to look on what was happening. Now they've started back up. They're chirping, singing, and flying around, which means that they're feeling comfortable again. That probably means that the poachers have moved a little ways off. Observation taken care of, I go to the next step.

A stands for Analyze: Papa says to ask yourself a few quick questions: Are you in immediate danger? Does the situation have the potential to become dangerous? What is it that you need to do to stay safe? I am out of immediate danger. Check. Now I just have the potential of being in a dangerous situation. The beaver could come back and be mad that I am in his lodge, or the poachers could come back and try to get me. But even worse, seeing as the poachers left, that means that they are heading straight back to the deer, to the field. That means that Dawn may be in immediate danger. That means I have to get out of this beaver lodge and back to her ASAP. This leads me straight to P.

P stands for Plan: What is my plan? Well, number one: get out of this beaver lodge. Number two: find Dawn. Two simple steps.

Last but not least, E stands for Execute. I have to execute my plan. I have to get out of this beaver lodge. I can't go out the entrance, seeing as it is underwater and is probably way too small for me to squirm through. I crawl over to the edge and start pushing at the branches, but it's built good and tight on the side. I don't want to do any more damage to this beaver's home, so I stop clawing at it and think of other ways. I look up and wonder if I could get out the way I came in without getting all scraped up again.

I can hear that old beaver thwapping his tail, and he is making some other noises, so I know he's somewhere nearby. I don't think he'll come in here, though, because he smells me and knows I'm here. But I swear, I'm not one hundred percent sure of that, and I'm seeing his big teeth and the branches he managed to chew through, and when I look down at my arm, it's not nearly as thick as most of what he has made his lodge out of.

I look back up at the top of this lodge. I stand up and the ceiling is about two inches above my head. I grab the biggest branch I can see, probably the limb that hit me right under my eye. And I pull up.

I've climbed a lot of trees, but there is something different about this. I can't put my feet anywhere. I am just supposed to pull myself straight up out of it. I'm wishing I had a pull-up bar in my room so I could've practiced for things like this.

I yank myself up so I can get my armpits on the sides of the hole and I hang there for minute, trying to catch my breath. I push all my weight into the palms of my hands, only then a branch breaks and my arm slides in up to my elbow and my hurt palm is getting scraped up on the rough bark, so I scramble back to the first position and just hang again.

I hear the beaver and I turn and see him sliding through the water and I don't know, but he looks a little bit frantic and little bit confused. About as confused as me, I guess. I tell myself to dig deep. I tell myself I've got to move fast or I'm going to fall back in. I push down on the tree limbs one more time and this time I push myself out up to my torso. Then I hear a little snap and throw myself like a log right over the edge and roll down the side of that beaver lodge.

I land in the pond and I tuck myself up against the bank in case there are any poachers left in the trees. I know I have a wild imagination. Dawn says it, Mama and Papa say it. Even Mr. Crock says it when I tell him a story or two. But right now I couldn't even dream up anything worse happening. I sit there in the sun as the beaver pops his head out of the water and gives my heart opportunity to start pounding again.

The arrow has floated my way and I grab it up out of the water before I can think twice. I point it at the beaver.

"I'm headed out of here," I tell him. Just to reassure him that he can go on back to bed now and when he wakes up I will be long gone. He seems to take the hint because he dives under the water and disappears.

I look around myself. I guess the best thing I can do is try and follow my trail back through the woods, but then I'll be going almost directly where the poachers have gone. *Still*, I think, tucking that arrow up under my armpit, *that's the way toward Dawn*. All of a sudden, I am moving faster.

I put my lips together and call through the trees, "*Feebee, feebee*."

Nothing comes back my way. The only thing worse than an RSDS is silence when there should be one. I hoof it.

Chapter Sixteen

I jump through tree limbs and over downed logs. It's doing this that I feel straight wrung out. But my mind isn't wrung out, it's going wild worrying about Dawn. I slow up as I get to the clearing, hold that arrow tight in my hand. If I come across those poachers again, I wouldn't think twice about putting this into a leg or an arm. I look out and see the deer blood, already turning a darker color. Already blending in among the red leaves around it. But the dead buck is gone from the edge of the forest and the men are too. I run around the side of the field.

"Feebee, feebee," I sing out, but still, nothing comes

back my way. I run until I see our backpack. The top is ripped open and the contents are spilling out along the ground. I run straight to it and start to look around at what's missing. Map, book, top hat, extra clothes. Most everything is still here. I figure I had better start tracking.

I look down and there's one set of tracks, and they are Dawn's for sure. I follow them one way, and I come to the edge of the field again. I see where she laid down— all of the grass is bent sideways and the leaves that are dried have just flaked into little pieces. And I see throw up too, so I know it was her and not some deer.

I watch the tracks. They loop around and go the other way, and I can tell she is moving fast because her prints become messy, tearing up the grass here and there. She must have gone after me. But why didn't I see her when I came from the pond?

I have so much going on in my head, I am not thinking straight. I stop right there and try to B.O.A.P.E. again. I feel my chest go up and down as I take a deep breath. As soon as I do this, my mind seems to clear. Mama says if you want to know what's on the ground, then you should go up.

I run over to the backpack and look inside for the binoculars. They're nowhere to be seen. Dawn must have taken them with her.

"*Feebee, feebee,*" I sing out again. This time, I think I hear the song of a blue jay, but I am not one hundred percent sure. I stick my arrow in the ground, and I put my foot on the lowest branch of a pine tree and start climbing. The bark burns my hand and I'm sure pus is oozing out of my splinters, but that's not really what I am thinking about right now. I'm thinking about getting as high as I can so I can see if Dawn is somewhere in the field. I want to see if the poachers are visible, and I want to make sure that they're not close by. I climb and climb. Some of the branches are as thick as Papa's arm and some are tiny as a baby finger. I try to avoid the little ones, but sometimes I have to rest a foot on one for a second and pull myself up higher. I pretend I'm light as a feather.

I'm running short of breath when I pull myself up onto a thick limb and take a seat. I look out toward the field. Nothing's there. Not a person, not an animal. Two crows are investigating the scene, but they haven't landed yet. They just circle in the sky, and I wish I had their kind of eyes.

I turn and look through the dense trees to the forest floor. I can only see glimpses through the branches, but I scan for the colors that Dawn is wearing. I look from the base of the tree out to a bare spot where I guess the pond might be. I see a few chipmunks wrestling for a nut and I see an abandoned nest in a branch close by.

"*Feebee, feebee.*" I whistle my loudest this time. I sing once, twice, and three times over. Then I hold my breath and listen.

"*Thweet, thweet.*" This time I am sure I hear the blue jay. I swing around to where I thought the noise was coming from. But I can't see through the branches. I shift and climb around and crane my neck around everywhere.

"*Feebee, feebee,*" I sing again and wait for her call. When it comes, I'm sure I am looking the right direction.

Just then, in the distance, out toward the pond, I see a tree start to shake. I know something is up because there is no wind here. I keep my eye on it and I almost want to laugh when Dawn's head pops around the side of it. I have never been so happy to see her in my entire life, and that's a fact. Of course, she was up off the ground too. No wonder I couldn't see her. I was looking in all the wrong places. Dawn waves to me and signals to the ground. I give her an A-OK sign and start climbing my way back down.

As soon as I get to the ground, I think for a minute of calling out her name, but instead I whistle and she whistles back until she's standing there right in front of me. She grabs me and hugs me.

"Maple, you did a brave thing back there. You're crazy and it was the stupidest thing you've ever done, but it was brave." She holds me out for a minute and then she gets the concerned look on her face. She pushes the skin under my eye and it stings like I got a javelin through my skull straight to the back of my head.

"God, Maple, what happened to you? Where did you end up? You look like you were in a car wreck."

My clothes are torn up good and I can feel that my face is bruised some.

"Fell into a beaver den," I whisper.

Dawn looks at me for a minute. "Well, thank God for that," she says and puts her arm around my shoulder. But then she spins around toward the field.

"Maple, we have to fix you up, but I want to get a little bit farther away from here. If you know what I mean. Just in case the poachers come back."

I nod and look up at the sky. I am feeling run-down. But the sun is tipping to the west now and the shadows are growing longer under the trees.

"I'm fine, Dawn, let's just get to the Wise Woman and get out of here."

But Dawn isn't really listening. She's throwing all of our stuff back into the backpack. She pulls the binoculars from around her neck and puts them in. She takes the compass from around my neck and puts it around hers instead. She sees the arrow that I left at the bottom of the tree and her eyes go wide.

"Where did you get that, Maple?"

"They shot it at me, Dawn, and I was scared coming back, so I grabbed it out of the pond."

Dawn gets up off her knees and takes my good hand.

"God, Maple. I heard a sound, but I wasn't sure. I didn't know—" Dawn says. She pulls my head into her and just starts hugging me again. Sort of like Mama would hug me, or Gramma, sort of like I would hug Beetle or the baby. An older person caring sort of hug. I lean and rest my head on her shoulder, happy to feel safe for the moment.

Chapter Seventeen

We dodge through the trees, and Dawn keeps looking over her shoulder and eyeing the shadows. I see she's trying to move fast out of there, but we start climbing a hill and I feel like for each step forward, I am sliding two feet back. I swear I can feel my heartbeat in every cut and bruise that I have. My body is thrumming like a scared partridge. As I climb, my lungs feel like they're on fire and my mouth is dry. I have to lick the insides of my cheeks to keep them from sticking to my teeth. Dawn is leading the way now, with both the backpack and the compass, and each step takes her farther away from me.

"Dawn, hang on," I gasp.

Dawn stops and comes back to me. She puts an arm around my waist and we climb up the hill. At the top, I stop and lean into her. And she holds me up, though I do notice her arm is shaking a little bit.

"Boy, Maple. You look like you have no energy left in you."

I give her a nod, but it is not all bad.

"I'm just feeling thirsty and a little bit tuckered. I am sure I'll do better if I have a quick break," I say.

Dawn looks over her shoulder and we walk across a flat area. We set up on one side of a big slab of rock. I look up at it, wishing it were the Wise Woman.

"Here." Dawn swings the backpack off her shoulders. "Let's get some water into you."

The water bottle has just a few sips left in it. I take two swallows and my whole body seems to wake right up. I look for a minute at the last little sip.

"You better have some too," I say and pass Dawn the bottle.

"Nope, I'm all set," she says and watches me drink the rest down.

Next, she pulls out the first-aid kit and starts fussing about the scrape under my eye. It hurts when she dabs at it. But the swab is covered in blood, wet and dry.

"Well, it's not too deep, Maple, but there is a huge

bruise swelling up around it." I can feel that, like there's a little bit of water in my cheek.

"We'd better cover it so no more germs can get in. We don't want this getting any worse than it already is." She dabs it with first-aid cream and then puts a little cotton piece on it and tapes it down. The tape reaches from my cheek up around my eye on both sides. Lucky I am not smiling or it would probably come right off.

Some branches managed to snag through my sweatshirt and pants. So we check the scrapes on my arms and legs. Nothing bad, just like I might have skidded off my bike and got some decent burns.

"Do you have any other bad ones, Maple?"

I don't even mean to do it, but without thinking, I flip my hand right over. My palm is red and swelling and the pus is back even though I thought I squeezed it all out trying to get out of that beaver den.

"Oh my God, what happened here?" Dawn says as she looks it over. "Maple, when did this happen? It looks like you have a bunch of splinters festering in there."

I try to think up a good story, but then I blurt out the truth.

"I got it when we were in the river. I hung on to the edge of the boat and it was all cut up and rough. I didn't want to tell you earlier because I thought you would see it and try and send us back with the ranger again."

Dawn's jaw tightens. "You're exactly right, I probably should have sent us with that park ranger. And we would have been spared the poaching and the near bear attack. You also would have been spared almost getting killed in a beaver den, and me having to explain this state of affairs to Mama and Papa. The only reason we aren't turning around now is because we're almost there."

I don't want to hear her speech right now, so I lay my head back in the dirt and rocks. I start to put my good arm over my eyes to block out the sun, but I realize there isn't really any sun left. I mean, it's not all gone, but it's getting later every second.

"Dawn, we gotta get going."

"No, we need to get some gauze on this." Dawn has the first-aid cream out and she is dabbing at my hand. "Exposure to dirt all day long obviously didn't help. You should have put some antiseptic on it and covered it right when we got to shore."

She drops the first-aid cream and picks up a ball of gauze. She wraps my hand, tears the gauze with her teeth and then tucks the end in against my skin and secures it with some tape.

"Thanks," I say and pretend to be real interested in the bandage. "That feels great, much better. Let's keep going."

Dawn tosses the first-aid kit back into the backpack

and it slides down next to the arrow, which is standing on end, poking out the top. Dawn swings the backpack to her back and turns with the compass to get a reading north.

"I really don't know how I'm going to explain this to Mama and Papa," Dawn says.

"I'll tell them all about it myself. Let's just keep on going," I say.

Dawn doesn't answer, and I suppose she's giving me the silent treatment. Or she's realizing just how right and smart I am. So we walk again through the trees and I have to try and go away in my mind. I'm thinking on waterfalls and rainbows. But then I realize how thirsty I am and I just keep thinking of some delicious water or maybe iced tea. We start walking across an open meadow and I pull up a piece of timothy and start chewing the end of it. Only it's dry and tastes like straw. I spit it out on the ground and walk behind Dawn, hoping like crazy that the Wise Woman is around the next bend.

Chapter Eighteen

I pull the hood of my sweatshirt up over my head and try and clamp it down over my ears.

"It's got to be over the next hill," Dawn pants.

I never knew my body could be so sore. Both of my feet feel like they're on fire. My arms and legs are getting heavier with every step. And my stomach is starting to growl like an angry dog.

I look up at Dawn leading the way, and I can tell she is tired because her steps are slower, and I see her legs shaking, but she's still pulling away from me.

"Dawn, wait up," I say, putting my hand to a tree to help pull me forward.

"Here, Maple." Dawn stops and moves to the side. "I want you . . . to go . . . in front," she pants. "That way . . . we go . . . at your pace."

She'll probably start complaining about how slow we're going, but as I pass her, I see genuine concern in her eyes, so I keep on going and she falls into step behind me.

As we come to the top of a hill, I cross my fingers. My eyes move ahead of me, expecting to see the Wise Woman. Expecting that she'll come shooting up out of the ground in front of me, but as I reach the top, my eyes dart back and forth. Nothing. Nothing except another hill to climb.

"I'm tired, Maple," Dawn says after she regains her breath. "I don't know, all this climbing—I'm getting worried."

We both look out at the horizon. The sun is nearing it. Drawing closer every minute.

"We need a distraction," I say, going forward.

"Yeah, but what?" Dawn says.

"I spy with my little eye—"

"No, I hate that game," Dawn says.

I start across a flat, rocky area and search my memory.

"It's okay. We can do something else. . . . What is . . ." *Think, Maple. Think.* "The Latin name for the great blue heron."

"*Ardea herodias*," she says before I even get the name out.

"Grosbeak?"

"Uhm . . . *Coccothraustes vesp* . . . *vespertinus.*"

I picture Papa's worn-out bird guide in my mind and try to flip through the pages.

"Dove," I say.

"*Columba livia.* Next."

"Hummingbird?"

"*Selasphorus*, oh, what is it? *Selasphorus* . . ."

"*Rufus*," I finish for her. We start a sharp ascent. This one almost looks like a little path. It almost looks like people have walked it before, not recently, but maybe at one time it was a well-used trail. It's rockier than the others. I try not to put my palm down, but it's tough to balance. I have to use it a little. The gauze gets dirty, but I am glad it's the gauze and not my palm.

"Good. Your turn. Cedar waxwing?" Dawn says.

"*Bombycilla cedrorum.*" I like this one because it sounds like drumbeats, beginning with *bom* and ending with a *rummmmmm.*

"Good. Hermit thrush?"

"*Catharus . . . guttatus*," I say. The names come faster as we move along.

"Red-winged blackbird?"

I can never pronounce this one. "*Angeli—*"

"Nope, *Agelaius phoeniceus*. There isn't an *n* in it," Dawn says.

"Right. I always forget. Mourning dove?"

"*Zenaida macroura*," Dawn says.

"Barn owl?"

"That one's easy," she says, and we say it together: "*Tyto alba*."

I am trying to move quickly up the hill in front of Dawn. But it's steep and my legs are burning and my breath is puffing out.

"Pheasant?" Dawn says.

"*Phasianus colchicus*." I am working the words around in my mouth when my foot slips out from under me. My hip lands hard on a root and I am sliding down toward Dawn: a human avalanche. The rocks scrape my thigh. I can feel the burn through my jeans. Dawn's eyes come at me big and wide.

"Watch out!" I say, digging my heels in hard. I spin up dirt and rocks.

"Stop!" Dawn screams and tries to step out of the way, but we are not far enough apart, and I'm moving like a waxed toboggan on icy snow. My feet hit her right in the shin and she topples over on me. I don't realize until I've stopped that I've used my hand as a brake. Pain shoots up my arm and I scream. I pull it out and stare at it. The gauze is just a little thread hanging loosely from my fingers. My hand is shaking like crazy and Dawn is holding her ankle.

"Oww," she says and just like that I lay back and drop my head in the dirt. I am done, she is done. Here we are screaming like a pack of coyotes and I wouldn't be surprised if we're about to get shot, lying on the side of this hill. We're both sore and weak and I don't feel like I could climb another step.

Dawn rolls over and pulls the backpack off her back. She drops the compass in and I watch it slide to the bottom as she pulls out the first-aid kit. She unclips the sides and takes out an ice pack and more gauze. She hands the gauze to me and cracks the cold pack.

"Jeez Louise," I say as I wipe the dirt off my palm. I undo the gauze and start lacing it around my hand and between my thumb and index finger.

I hear Dawn's whistley breath. It gets louder when she is worried and right now she sounds like a chimney full of wind. I am about to tell her to please knock it off when I see a little spark out of the corner of my eye. It's the monarch. I had forgotten all about it, but there it is fluttering over to us. It lands right on my shoulder. I tear the gauze with my teeth and tuck it against my palm. The monarch flits and flutters off my shoulder and up the path. I pull myself up.

"C'mon, Dawn. We really need to get going. It's getting dark. Can you walk?"

"Yeah, I think I twisted my ankle a little bit," she says and rolls her foot from one side to the other. "I should be all right. Let me see your hand. That bandage looks really loose."

The butterfly flits up over the hill.

"I'm all set," I say and grab the backpack off the ground and swing it to my back.

"Maple, are you hiding something? Let me see it."

But I jump up the trail after that butterfly. It disappears quickly over the hill. I don't stop or go back, I just keep on climbing, getting a hunch somewhere that just over this hill I will find what I am looking for. I scramble up the trail on hands and knees. I crouch like a catamount and move fast over the ground. The gauze gets dirty real fast, but I don't care, I keep climbing, hand over hand. Some rocks slide out from under my feet and I fall, but I dig my toes into the earth and push forward.

"Maple, wait!" Dawn yells, but I can't stop. If I stop, I won't start again.

"Just wait there—I'll be right back," I holler over my shoulder. My heart pounds and my eyes tear. But I have to get there before nightfall. We have to get home. Finally, my hand swings into open space.

I teeter at the top of the hill. I search for the Wise Woman. For a pool of miracle water.

But there's nothing here.

Nothing but some shrubs, and a weeping willow with branches kissing the moss at its feet.

Chapter Nineteen

No!" I tear the backpack from my shoulders and throw it down the hill. It tumbles and the map and book and arrow fly out of it. The book spins, pages turning. "This isn't fair!" I scream into the trees and start running, but something catches, and the world twists like a woodland merry-go-round. Around and around the forest spins, green and gold. The colors flicker. My body twists. Everything fades.

The first thing I hear when I come around is the *dripdripdrip* of water. I think for a second that I'm dreaming. But as the treetops come into view, I remember where I am. Failing on my journey, that's where. I put my hand in the moss that I have landed in. I stagger to my feet. The glen is filling with shadows and golden sunset, and I lean against the weeping willow and make myself stand.

I try to shake that water noise out of my ears, but it just keeps on. My heart gives my chest a kick. Don't get all excited, I tell myself. Could be nothing, like it has been all day. Still, I move quickly. I follow the sound of the water. I have lost my shoes and my feet press into the moss. It's squishy between my toes.

I walk around the willow, around the twisting vines and high shrubs, and the moss grows cooler under my feet. As I turn the corner, she greets me. A face, jumping straight out of the earth, made of rock. The sun is slanting and throws long fingers of orange light through the treetops and down onto her cheeks. It's her. The Wise Woman.

I put my splintered hand to my head and move forward without realizing. I stand on soft moss and sink in, rocking back and forth. Vines tangle down from above and tickle her face like curls. And that sort of makes me think of my mama.

I have never seen a stone cry before, but there she is, water running down her face like tears and collecting in what looks like a set of giant hands.

I step closer and put my hands on hers, my fingertips resting in the water. The water is not how I pictured it. The water I imagined shimmered like the northern lights: it had glints of rose quartz and opal. Instead, it feels the same as the pond water. It looks the same too, only the fountain has collected algae. Green sludge slides down the sides. But I try and ignore that, because I've never seen miracle water before, so maybe this is what it looks like.

"I am so glad I found you," I whisper. The sun winks from its spot on the horizon and the Wise Woman's face blinks, like fireflies live under her rocky skin.

I bow my head.

"My God," Dawn says as she hops around the bend. "When I saw our bag there on the ground—I had no idea where you were. I . . . was . . . scared to death."

The open backpack hangs from her arm. She's still holding the ice pack in her other hand, but when she sees the Wise Woman she stops in her tracks and drops the bag and the ice pack on the ground.

"We made it?" she whispers and falls to her knees at my side.

"Yes," I say, "we made it."

"We made it," she says. She turns around and grabs the backpack. She pulls the empty water bottle from it and hands it to me. Then she puts her arm around my shoulder. Here we sit at the Wise Woman's fountain. Exhausted, worn down, shaking. But together, and whole, and about to bring our baby sister a miracle. I think of the long day, and my aching body, and how everything is going to be worth it if we can just get home and give this bottle to the baby. I picture Mama smiling down at me. Papa patting me on the back. Beetle giving me a warm hug. I imagine the baby gaining strength. I imagine her running with us through the yard, breathing in the healthy mountain air. I imagine birthdays, holidays, and the celebrations of all the seasons. In the summer, I'll show her the raspberry bushes and the vegetables in the garden. In the fall, I'll show her the colorful leaves and the best place to find the brightest trees. In the winter, I'll teach her how to sled without falling right out into the snow, and I'll bring her for a fast ride in our toboggan. And in the spring, I'll show her how to make pure maple syrup, just like Mama and Papa showed me. I'll watch her taste that first sap and then the rich boiled-down version. Just like I did with Beetle. Just like big sisters are supposed to do. There are so many things to look forward to. I dip the bottle into the fountain. The water is frigid.

"We're coming, Lily, we're coming," I whisper.

I think back to Mama tucking me into bed at night and the words ring in my soul:

> *Please, Wise Woman,*
> *Have mercy on me.*
> *Grant me a miracle*

If pure my soul be.
Grant me this wish,
I ask of you.
Grant me this wish
My intention is true.

"This water is for our baby sister. She is very sick and fragile, and we want her to get healthy and strong. So please, Wise Woman, grant me this miracle. Keep our baby sister alive."

I pull the bottle out of the water. Some algae has made its way in, and it swirls as the water settles.

Dawn eyes it and then looks at me with her eyebrows sort of pulling toward center. I don't ask her what she's thinking, but she tells me anyway.

"That doesn't look very good. It looks like something that could give you giardia," she says.

"Yeah," I say, "but Remington didn't get giardia, he got better. Let's not worry about what it looks like."

Dawn pinches her lips and nods. "I suppose," she says.

One last thing to do. I think back on Mama telling me the tale. I hold the water bottle tight in my fist and stare into the pool.

"We are supposed to read what is written in the pool," I say.

Dawn grimaces and reaches her hand into the water.

She slides her hand along the bottom and chunks of algae
float up around her wrist.

"Oh, that is just lovely," Dawn says.

The water fogs up with green and brown murkiness.
I put the water bottle down gently at my side and slide
my hand in to help. I scoop up a gob of algae and throw
it on the ground. I do this probably ten times or more
and Dawn is helping too, and I wish we had one of those
nets that fancy Lauren Roberts has to clean her pool. But
we don't, so we just keep on skimming.

"It says 'Read and understand,'" Dawn says as she
stops and squints down into the water. She pushes her
hand back down into the bottom of the pool and I watch
the dwindling light bounce and reflect on her wrist. Her
hand looks chalky white, almost blue under the water.

"I can't read the rest," she says.

The algae is cleaned out, but the words are chopped
up, like word ruins, really, more than words.

```
READ AND UNDERSTAND
L  E AND        U    LOVE
H A S THE WO   DS OF MAN
L  E  ND LOVE    PURE  L V
    MIRACL     HA D.
```

"I can make out a few of the words," I say.

Dawn pulls her hand out of the water and shakes it

off and I scrape at the empty spaces, to make sure there isn't any more algae there. The blank spaces remain the same.

"'Has the words of man' could be the second sentence," I say.

"That makes no sense," Dawn says.

I try to hold back from rolling my eyes at her.

"The last one says 'miracle had,'" Dawn says.

"That can't be right either," I say.

She puts her hand on her chin.

"So all we have is, 'Love and you love, has the words of man. Love and love, pure love—'"

"'Miracle had.'" Dawn frowns. "Well, it's all we've got and we're running out of time."

I pick the water bottle back up. Dawn and I grab onto it and raise it above our heads. The rosy sunlight sparkles through and reflects pink pixie-beams on the Wise Woman's face.

We stumble along: "'Love and you love, has the words of man. Love and love, pure love, miracle had.'"

Nothing changes, except some algae floats around in the bottom of the bottle.

"Do you think that worked?" Dawn asks.

"I don't know," I say. "But we have the water, and that's the miracle. Remember Remi and Uncle Meyers?"

"All right, let's get going, then," Dawn says.

"Okay," I say. "Thank you, Wise Woman. I am sorry

for our quick visit, but you understand, we have to get home . . . before it's too late."

I kiss the edge of her giant hand, and Dawn does the same, only she barely touches the stone with her lips.

"You ready?" Dawn says.

"Yeah," I say. I look once more toward the Wise Woman. She peers out at me. As I stare, her cheeks flash red and all of a sudden the shadows are fuller, darker. The day colder. I look through the trees and out to the horizon. The sun disappears and leaves a dark line, like a frown, lying across the mountain. A chickadee sings its last call through the treetops. *Warning*, it says. *Warning*.

Chapter Twenty

I lean up against the weeping willow and push my feet back into my shoes one at a time. A blister has formed on my right heel and it breaks as I slide my shoe on. The open wound feels bigger than it is. Leaves skitter across the ground. They sound like feet, running, chasing around us. I try to Velcro my shoe, but seem to be having a hard time controlling my muscles. My hand jumps around so much, I can't line the stripes up right. I breathe into my belly, trying to remain calm. The edges finally match and I clamp it down tight.

Dawn digs her hand into the backpack and pulls out the Maglite. She clicks it on and I see her breath billow out into the beam. She limps over and picks up *Mountain Legends* from its spot on the forest floor. She shoves it into the backpack, then picks up the map and moves over to me.

The wind kicks up for a minute, and I pull my hood over my head and huddle against myself. *I'm not afraid of the dark,* I say to my jumping soul. At least at home I'm not. Here in the middle of the woods, the sun sets and the night comes alive with howlers.

"I guess we have two choices," Dawn says. "We either stay here and build a fire—"

"Or we walk out," I say. My body is telling me to stay still. But the miracle water is in my hand and even though it doesn't look the way I thought it would, it still reminds me of the baby, waiting. Of how much pain *she* must be in.

"We might already be too late. I don't want us to risk being any later," I say. The memory of the poachers flashes in my mind, and my skin crawls at the sound of the forest coming alive. "We should keep going."

Dawn's gaze darts around the trees, beyond the beam of the Maglite and into the shadows.

"I have to admit, Maple, I want to go too, but I don't know the best way out of here. My ankle is aching as well."

"I'm feeling the same," I say. "I mean, worn down."

I start thinking we could stop to make a fire and wait, but then my mind starts thinking of bones. The animals that are howling in the trees picking our bones. Maybe the park ranger stumbling upon our bones. The sun and rain and weather bleaching and doing their best to disappear our bones.

"We made it here together. We can figure this out," I say. We have to. We don't have any other choice.

Dawn shines the flashlight onto the map in her hand, and I feel the shadows crash in around us. Dawn must too; her breath quickens.

"There's gotta be a road nearby," I say.

Dawn puts an index finger on the Wise Woman. The flashlight beam bounces and shakes across the page, but my eyes focus.

"Kilgery Lane," I say, putting a finger down on the road. "We must know someone on Kilgery Lane."

Dawn ducks in closer. "It looks like it's about a half mile west of here," she says.

"Okay. That's doable," I say. "That's probably our quickest route."

"Okay," she says. "Which way is west?"

I put the miracle water in the pocket of my hoodie and grab the backpack from Dawn's feet. I search the inside for the compass. I reach down toward the bottom where I am sure it went. My fingers look for the leather

lacing, but all I feel is the top hat, the book's sharp corners, the head of the arrow, and my jacket, still damp
from this morning.

"C'mon, Maple, we don't have all day," Dawn says
as she pushes the flashlight beam into the backpack and
breathes into her other hand. I push *Mountain Legends* to
the side. No compass. I rip open the front, in case Dawn
moved it when I wasn't with her. There is nothing there
but a couple of tea bags from when we went camping
last.

"Maple, where is the compass? I put it in here. When
we were on the hill. When I twisted my ankle. Where
is the compass?" Her voice is rising and I put my finger
to my lips.

"Dawn, quiet," I whisper, eyeing the shadowy trees.
"This is the worst possible time to be making noise."

She rips the bag out of my hands and dumps the
contents on the mossy ground. She shines the flashlight
over it.

It's not here.

I swallow hard. "It—it must have bounced out when
I, when I tossed the bag," I say.

"Oh God," Dawn says, and a second later the flashlight beam becomes a searchlight, bouncing through the
trees. It circles and stops and circles again. I try to keep
up with it and run out to where I fell. I feel around on

the moss with my hands, pushing leaves out of the way. It must have been covered. It must be lying right here. But my fingers sink into the soft earth. My fingertips, growing numb from the cold, barely pick up the dampness of the moss, the sharp edges of the leaves. But surely I would *see* the compass. Dawn comes to stand next to me again, and we both jump as a coyote screams through the treetops.

"We gotta get out of here," Dawn says.

I stand up and try to think. Where could that compass be? Where could it be?

"We don't have a compass," Dawn says. "We don't have a compass." She breathes in through her nose and out through her mouth. "There're other ways." She limps back to the backpack, leaving me in nothing but moonlight. I run to catch up and we pile our things back into the pack. Dawn secures it to both shoulders.

"The sun set over there, so that must be west," she says.

Yes, the sun rises in the east and sets in the west. I stare through the trees and plant my eyes on the horizon.

Dawn and I fall into step beside one another. Dawn pans the ground with the light and my eyes dart back and forth into the shadows, wondering what is there. We have the miracle. We are together. We are safe. I say this over and over in my head.

I hunch my shoulders against the cold. The wind

picks up, and the dead branches snap like bones against one another. Dead leaves whip up into our faces and across our arms and legs as though they want to bury us underneath them. I feel Dawn's arm shaking and I am sure she can feel mine. And we lean against each other, holding each other up. We step across moss. Now more than ever, quiet as a catamount. Clever as a fox. Quiet as a catamount. Clever as a fox.

Chapter Twenty-one

Ikeep my eyes on the western mountain. I keep my heart pointed toward home. We have walked out of the wood line and are working our way across an open field. And we are moving slow. The grass is tall, and I don't look down, afraid of what might be resting in it. Snakes . . . big spiders that only come out at night. Rodents.

"Do you hear that?" Dawn says as she cocks her head to the side.

My heart lurches into my throat. Do I hear what? Coyote? Poachers hunting for humans? A bear, back for revenge? A mountain lion lurking in the dark?

"What?" I say.

She shakes her head. "I must be going crazy. Distract me."

I try and clear my head. "All right, Latin name for moorhen."

Dawn scowls. "Did we learn that one?"

"Yeah," I say. "It was one of the first ones."

"I don't remember," she whispers.

"*Gallinula chloropus*," I say.

"How did you remember that?" she says. "That was a long time ago."

I just shrug my shoulders. But I can't help but notice that she complimented me. She actually complimented me for the first time in, well, I don't know how long.

"How about the common sandpiper?" I ask, stepping over an abandoned tree branch. Carried here, maybe, by a strong wind, or I don't know what, but it's looking spooky in the moonlight. And I jump as a tiny little twig tickles my knee.

"*Actitis hypoleucos*," Dawn says as I help her over the branch. "I remember that one." She stops in the grass. "I keep thinking that I hear something." Her voice is high and shaky. I hear a lot of different noises, but there is *something* that seems closer than the rest.

Dawn whirls around with the flashlight, and I almost want to close my eyes rather than see what is there. I spin Dawn to the side and pull that arrow right out of our backpack. I hold it straight out and brace myself for a bear fight.

I squint in the moonlight and my ears are alert to all the forest scufflings. But I don't see a thing. Not at first, anyway. Dawn shines the flashlight as far out as it will go and all of a sudden, just where the beam ends, the grass begins to fold over, as though something is cutting through it, toward us. I imagine there is a genuine lion slinking up careful. I aim my arrow.

"What is it?" Dawn says. The beam of the flashlight begins to bounce as we step back a foot. It jostles and pitches, and spills right out of Dawn's hand. The flashlight lands in the grass and illuminates a set of beady eyes coming straight underneath the branch we just crossed. I throw the arrow without even thinking. I shoot it out like a hand grenade. But it thuds into the ground ten feet from us. And the creature keeps on coming and as it steps closer, there is no doubt in my mind what it is. I see a pointy little nose and I smell the most awful of smells. Skunk. His hair is standing up on end and his tail is pointed toward heaven.

"Oh God!" Dawn shouts, and her hand goes up to her nose.

"Run!" I holler. I move to the right and Dawn to the left and we nearly collide. Then Dawn darts out in

front of me. Even though she is limping and I'm cut and
sore, we run like ninjas, feet hitting the ground, blisters
and burning forgotten. The air is cold and I can feel the
stinging in my ears. I am breathing ice into my lungs.
But I keep up, and Dawn and I crash like a herd of deer
into the trees. We don't stop. We move in and out of
the shadows. We dodge trees and run until the smell
fades. Then, just like that, my feet catch on something
and both Dawn and I are sprawling forward. My feet
feel like they're pulled straight out of my ankle sockets.
I reach back and feel around. It's a big old root meant
to do harm. I look over at Dawn and I see her biting
her lip.

"My ankle," she says, huffing. I see the breath come
out of her nose in little gray puffs.

"Did you twist it again?" I whisper.

"Worse, I think," she says as she sits up and feels it
with her fingertips. "I think I heard something pop." She
reaches a hand out to me. I stand up and then I pull
her up, but as soon as she sets a little weight on it, she
crumples to the ground.

"I don't think I can keep going," Dawn says, and
though it's dark, though our flashlight is gone, the silver
moonlight that cuts through the trees is enough to let me
see her tears. I don't hold back, then. I start crying too.

"Maybe they'll send a search party," I whisper, but

I'm scared now, dead scared and trying to figure out what to do.

"Maybe." Dawn's fingers are cold in mine.

"Maybe we should scream for help," I say. "Maybe some people are out looking for us. Maybe they're over the next hill and are waiting for us to call out?"

Dawn breathes in and wipes her nose. Then she stops and her eyes go wide.

"What is it?" I'm almost afraid to ask. My insides feel like they have turned into pudding.

"Shhhhh," Dawn says and starts crawling along the forest floor.

"What?" I whisper.

Please, no more skunks, no coyotes, no nothing. Please be a search party. Please be annoying Trevor Collins and his dad.

But it's none of these things.

It's not a senseless animal. It's not a park ranger, or a search party. There are voices among the trees. Gruff, familiar voices in the night.

Chapter Twenty-two

The leaves and twigs stick my chest as I slide forward to hide next to Dawn, and the plastic of the water bottle crinkles in my front pocket. I tell it to be silent and make myself still as stone. When I look out, I can't believe what I am seeing. First, I see two lanterns lit, and I search the area, looking for figures.

"Damnit! Yeeeoooo. . . . That one tried to get away from me. Not in a million years, pretty birdie," a man says as he steps out from behind a tree. My stomach goes sour, like I ate too many green currants. Dawn's fingers tighten on a tree root and she seems to have stopped breathing. It's them. The poachers. I can't be sure, but I think I see the muzzle of a gun this time. It sits comfortably on the man's back and kisses the rim of his hat. I see a strap reach around his chest. No mistake. He's got a rifle now. He turns toward a lantern, and the already dark paint on his face mixes with shadows and makes big sunken holes where his eyes should be. A fluffy white owl hangs from his hand. Its eyes are dead and distant. Blood runs over its white feathers, down its leathered legs, and across the man's thick wrist.

"Leroy, come take a look at this beaut," he says into the trees.

The other man walks into the clearing. His gun is raised to his eye and he points it to the wood line, to where we hide. The hair on the back of my neck is standing up on end now.

"Thought I heard somethin'," he says.

"If it ain't hooting, we don't want it, Leroy. You keep that in mind now. Don't go getting all trigger happy, okay?"

Nighttime owl killers. Cowards. The first one throws his owl in a pile. I try to pretend this isn't happening, that if I look away and back, they'll be gone. I look down at my shaking hands, at the pine needles that poke through my fingers, but as soon as I glance into the glen again, I know I'm not dreaming.

"I keep thinking I am hearing things, Jim. I keep thinking I'm hearing things in the woods. Screams, I

thought. Not coyote calls, but genuine screams. You
don't reckon . . ." He stops talking, puts his rifle down,
and picks up a lantern.

"Don't reckon what?" Jim says.

"Ach, it's nothing . . ." But he blows the lantern out,
making them darker and scarier than ever. He sits down
on a rotting log.

"Don't reckon what, Leroy? What'd you do that for?"
Jim says as he shoves a bloody cluster of feathers into a
sack.

"Well, you hear 'bout those girls? Supposedly ran off
into the mountains today? No one's sure where they are,
and . . ."

"What of it?"

"Well, supposing folks are out looking for them?
Supposing there is a whole search party out there
right now? We don't want to be drawing attention to
ourselves."

"I see what you're saying, Leroy. But if I promise someone genuine owl feathers, then I'm going to bring them
genuine owl feathers. I got mouths to feed, you know."

I tighten my grip on the roots and pine needles. The
dead autumn leaves rustle underneath me. The one called
Leroy spits something onto the forest floor, and I can't
see it well in the light, but I guess it might be phlegm or
tobacco or something. Then he keeps on yakking. "I say

we head back to town." He juts his chin out toward large shadows, a rusty old pickup.

Back to town. The words bounce around my head like an echo in the mountains.

"You yellow-bellied coward," Jim says. "I bring you out here to earn some money for you and Marge and you haven't been one lick of help the whole damn time."

"Right, sorry, Jim. I do appreciate it." Leroy goes silent. Jim picks up the lit lantern and he and Leroy move away from us toward the pickup. I feel the darkness crawl up my back. I feel my body, tired and sore, and I see Dawn up close. Twigs sit on her face, stuck to her tear tracks. I feel the water bottle jabbing into my side and I feel the *thump thump thump* of my heartbeat in my bruised-up hand.

"That's it," I whisper. My feet are already stretching into the ground. My calves getting ready to run.

Dawn looks at me and shakes her head. The moon and trees plant a jagged shadow across her face. It looks like a claw and seems to scrape her away as she shakes her head from side to side. "I don't know what you're thinking, Maple T. Rittle, but if it is what I think it is, then you better get that thought out of your head right this minute."

My throat twists like tree roots that have stood too long together.

"Don't you dare," Dawn whispers. "Do you have any·

idea how much trouble we'll be in if they catch us? They're poachers, Maple. They could kill us."

I see the one man, Jim, fling the sack of owls into the back of the pickup. It lands and rolls down the handle of a shovel, disappears behind the tailgate. The doors of the pickup creak as they pop open, and creak again as they slam shut. I hear the rumble of the engine.

"This is our ticket, Dawn," I whisper.

"Maple, I don't think I can get in there. My foot. I don't see how we can do it."

"I don't see any other choice, Dawn. You can't walk this way. I can hardly stand, myself. I'll help you," I say and start across the forest floor. Dawn shakes her head, but she pulls herself along next to me. And we come up below the bumper. "I'm hurt. I'm tired, and so are you. We can stay here and die trying to walk out, or we can get a ride back to town."

I hear the gears shift. The smell of exhaust hits me full in the face. My eyes sting. Dawn hunches down next to me. Her eyes are wide, and her nostrils poke out. The taillights pick up the beads of sweat on her head. "You're crazy," she whispers, "but you're right."

I get ready to argue, but then the words settle, and it takes me a moment to register what's happened. I'm right?

"It's about time we got home," Dawn says.

I don't say a word. I just nod, readjust the water in

the center of my sweatshirt pocket and place my hands on the bumper. I lift myself slowly and peek over the tailgate.

Bags, gear, and guns lean up against the cab window. I'm thinking they'll be plenty enough to shield us from view. I grab Dawn's hand.

"Put your weight on me and lift your good foot to the bumper."

Dawn leans on me and places her foot on the bumper. Her sore ankle is barely pressing into the ground. The truck makes a lurch forward, but I am ready and I give her a push and she flips over the tailgate and out of view. The whole truck is jostling now, out across roots and rocks. I sneak along behind it as fast as I can. I grab onto the tailgate with the tips of my fingers and swing over it fast. I throw myself low, my knees colliding with the cold metal, the bottle jamming into me, taking away my breath. My chin smacks down hard. Pain shoots through my head. I freeze until my breath comes again, and listen for a word from the front, for a sign that they know we're here. Nothing.

I lean up and notice Dawn covering her mouth with her hand and kinda lurching forward like she is throwing up. Only nothing is coming out. I feel something soft on my fingers. Velvety soft. A sour smell hits my nose, and when I look, I see the cause for her sickness. Dead eyes stare out at me. I gag, and I gag again and again. I

163

have landed between the front and hind legs of the dead
buck. The gutted buck. I cover my palm with the sleeve
of my sweatshirt and hold it over my nose.

The truck seems to moan, and it bounces out over
the rough ground. I see Dawn grab her stomach and look
out at the trees and she shakes her head and I shake mine
too and we both stare out the back. We sit up against the
dead owls in their brown body bags, I on one side of the
dead buck and Dawn on the other.

The ride is rough, the ground uneven. My jaw
bounces and hits my teeth against one another. Even
though I know the stars aren't moving around in the sky,
to me they seem to bounce like lightning bolts, across the
moon and into the trees. I listen to the coyotes scream
in the distance. Listen to my own heart pounding my
rib cage. And I've never been so scared before in all my
life, so I go away in my head and I start thinking on the
day. I start thinking on hopeful things, on miracles, and
my mind goes straight to that monarch butterfly. I start
remembering other miraculous times.

Mama hurried through the front door.

*"This is something my girls must see," she said as she flipped the
TV off.*

*We followed Mama out onto the porch. You wouldn't believe
the sight if I told you. Dawn held on to Beetle, and Dawn and I*

stood with our shoulders pressed together and our faces up in sheer wonder. At first I thought it was a mess of twirling autumn leaves. But when I spotted one of those leaves up close, I realized it was a genuine monarch butterfly. They were fluttering everywhere. They were moving around like loose leaves in a rainstorm. I saw Papa standing out in the middle of it. I stepped right in too, feeling the lightest breeze I ever did feel right on my cheeks and neck and hands.

We all just stood there with our arms stretched out, watching those golden wings flutter and shimmer in the sunlight. But before long, the cluster separated and started out across the river and through the yard until we couldn't see them anymore.

"Are they all right, Mama?" I asked.

Mama smiled and patted me right on the top of my head.

"Oh, they're not just all right, they're great, baby. They're going on an adventure."

"They are?" I said.

"These butterflies are migrating, baby. They're moving south for the winter."

My eyes went wide 'cause I could barely believe it. Butterflies couldn't hold up like that. Could they? How would they know where they were going? Their wings were all weak and covered in powder. Wouldn't they get nabbed off by predators one by one?

"Will they make it, Mama?" I asked as we walked back up the stairs and into the warm dining room.

"Monarchs are stronger than they look, baby," Mama said, "and they have a powerful sense how to get where they are going, even if

*they have never been there before. And how to get home, for that
matter. They've got intuition in their wings. They're not just beautiful. They're resilient, strong, and smart, especially when traveling
together."*

The truck jolts to a halt, and I slide on the pickup bed
and press myself to one of the brown bags. The front
legs of the deer jam into my lower back. I smell soil,
gunpowder, and something foul . . . death? I lift my
chin to see where we are. We've stopped, but we aren't
in town. No sign of the post office, no general store, no
white gazebo. I don't see Mr. Miller's carpentry shop on
the corner, or the firehouse with its shiny trucks. I scan
the ground and finally focus. The river. I see our canoe
standing against a tree where we left it. I see the puddle
where Curious lapped up some water. I see our own
tracks in the sand. There is only one difference from
the way it looked earlier in the day: the taillights bleed,
seeping onto the sand, imprinting our footprints with
a fresh coat of red. The waves of the Devil's Washbowl
lick out of the river like hungry tongues covered in
blood.

Chapter Twenty-three

Get under this," Dawn whispers and holds up a flannel jacket. It smells like mildew and eggs. She shoves it over my head, and a second later I am lying with my cheek against the torn up metal of the truck bed. I open the flannel a tiny bit so I can see out, so I can breathe. If I put my arms under my head, I can see Dawn above the buck's emptied stomach. And that is where I stare, above the rotting belly, to my sister. She throws a hunting vest over her head and leans a pair of boots up against her legs. I see her fingers lift the vest up slightly, her nose and mouth barely visible, but her face and her expression are pure shadows. The truck begins to jostle side to side and my stomach is flipping around like it has a monkey inside it.

"Make it quick, Leroy." The passenger door creaks open and slams shut. The whole truck shakes. Something tumbles softly and a second later a set of blank owl eyes stare back at my own. I bite my tongue so I don't scream and I hear a gasp from Dawn.

"Make it quick? I'll take as long as I please. When you gotta go, you gotta go," Leroy mutters as his footsteps crunch away. Please, please hurry. I stare back at the baby owl. If seeing an owl in broad daylight is bad luck, I don't want to think about what being in the company of a dead baby owl and a gutted buck might mean.

I try to still my thoughts, but they are flying around in my head. How did we get back here? Back to the where we started? I remember the logging roads we crossed and passed, the tire tracks that I thought could only be Mr. Collins's.

I hear a radio in the cab come on. It flips from station to station until it finally lands on a song.

"Oh yeah, 'Tuesday's Gone.' Boy is she," Jim says. The strong smell of smoke hits my nose, and I am think-ing it must be a cigar because I smelled a cigar before when Uncle Roy smoked one. I didn't like it then, and I sure don't like it now. It gets even worse a minute later because just as the piano music is ending, Jim starts singing and moaning along with the vocals: "Won't you please take me far away?"

"Oh my God," I hear Dawn whisper. "Can't they get on with it?"

Above the sound of the river and music, I hear a crunch of leaves. Footsteps. They grow louder and then quieter as Leroy walks from the woods back onto the sandy beach.

"What the heck is this? Let's listen to some country," he says. I hear his footsteps come around the truck to my side, to the side where the river rolls.

"Oops, we tipped our owl bag," he says quietly.

A big hairy hand floats down in front of my face. My breathing stops. The wind drops out of the trees and the radio flips to silence. The hand covers the little owl and drags it out of my line of vision.

"Almost got away from us," he says. I feel the owl bag pull away from me, giving me more room. A breeze tickles the hair around my ears.

"There we are now. Hey, what the hell's this?" A second later, I feel a gruff hand on the top of my head. The string of my hat tightens around my throat like a noose. And then I am moving out from under my shelter. Up into the moonlight. A big arm is wrapping itself around me. Around my waist and arms. The string on my hat breaks and it disappears from my head, from its clamp on my windpipe and I scream. I scream like I could split myself open with the sound.

He smells rotten and sour and I jerk one arm free of his grip and swing at him with my fist.

"What's going on out there?" Jim gets out of the truck, but before he can make it around, Dawn is flying out from under the hunting vest. Pushing off with some sort of mighty strength, she jumps straight at us.

"Don't touch my sister!" she screams and we all tumble backward. I fall over the poacher, to the edge of the river, across the sand, then into the water. The bottle of miracle water flies from my pocket and spins into the river, spins in the current and holds steady against a rock. Dawn falls over me and rolls among the rocks and lands with a splash next to the water bottle. I scramble toward her. From behind me, Jim's voice bangs out across the rapids: "Don't move."

Dawn is into the river up to her waist. I see her eyes go big. I wonder if there's a shotgun barrel aimed at the back of my head, or if she feels the river getting stronger.

"On your feet." On hands and knees, I turn toward the men. They're dark figures in the moonlight. I dunk a hand into the cold water and push myself upright. The bottle of miracle water spins around in a shallow eddy. I look toward Dawn. She raises herself out of the water like an injured fawn, her foot sitting strange on the rocks.

A second later, panic rises into her eyes. She slips to the side. The rocks, they're covered in algae. My feet slide on them too, no matter how I try to control my legs.

Dawn screams and the water bottle spins in the current. My eyes are darting from one to the other. My body tenses like a catamount ready to pounce, and then, as though sucked like a vacuum, both water bottle and Dawn crash away from me—the water bottle toward the center of the river and Dawn down onto hard rocks. I dive without thinking. Dive to save a sister. Dive to save a family.

"Move, Leroy. Go, go." I hear footsteps on the shore, doors slam as I grab onto Dawn's fingers. Her body straightens into the river. Her face becomes pale as the truck races away, leaving us in the cold moonlight. Dawn's fingers slip until the very tips are in my hand.

"The water!" Dawn screams. Her hand squirms as though she is trying to loosen herself from my hold. "We have to get the water!"

"Dawn! No, please." My heart hits my chest, hits the rocks that I lay on. Booms out into the current.

"Maple." Dawn's face is covered in water or tears or something. "The water." Her eyebrows come down in the center. But the bottle looks so ordinary as it bobs away from us. *I choose you,* I think. *Not a bottle of water.* The rocks under me loosen, give way. And the more I try and dig in, the more rocks skitter into the current. The wind whips up and leaves spin around us in a whirlwind.

"Hang on!" I scream as the last of the rocks disappear, filter out from under me. Dawn and I whip into the rapids. Into the cold dark. I close my eyes and shut my mouth tight. The sound of waves fills my ears, pumping rapids back and forth like the Devil's chant: *Washbowl. Washbowl.* Satan's fingers rise up out of the current. I scramble. But the waves are made of muscle. My feet twist and the water sucks me down. I cling to Dawn's fingers. *Just hang on,* I think, but the waves tear us apart. As her fingers let go, I open my eyes, see the stars for a moment, see the sky flash colors, and then the world sinks into darkness.

Chapter Twenty-four

Green and blue swirls dance like prayer flags across the sky. Not heaven, just northern lights. It's so cold. My joints are made of ice. I try to move, try to get up off the dead autumn leaves. The pains shooting through my body seem to make my mind sharp. Everything spills back at me. The guns, the water, Dawn. Tears spill out of my eyes, mix with the water that has already soaked my face, my clothes, and my skin. My body is shaking, trembling like the last leaf on a snow-covered bough.

"Dawn," I yell, only my voice comes out of me like a tiny peep. Not strong like I want it to be. I curl up into a sitting position. My stomach spasms and I throw up in the sand. Breathe, I tell my lungs, just stinking breathe.

"Dawn?" The water licks the tips of my toes as I search the shadows. I lurch forward, my bare feet sliding in throw up. I scramble through rocks and sand.

"Dawn, Dawn!" I rush along the bank, tearing up my palms and knees. "Dawn?"

My shoulder screams, feels loose and uncontrollable. It wobbles weakly and aches as I lean my weight against it. I push myself upright and tumble through bushes. My ankle snags and I fall forward onto the rocks. Something sour hits my throat and I stop again, curled over against a tree. I empty myself of water, more and more water. But the whole time, I keep screaming, spitting.

"Dawn. Answer me!"

I wipe the vomit from my lip and look up. The trees seem to swim in front of me. I fall backward onto weak ankles and knees. Clutch my heart with my hand. There she is. Dawn. One shoe off, one shoe on. Facedown in the sand. Her arms set sideways at awkward angles.

"Dawn," I whisper, my words puffing out of my mouth like a ghost.

I slide toward her. I push myself along the ground. Dig into the rocks and twigs where she lies. Her arms are so cold. The night is so cold. I turn her slowly. Her head rolls against my arm. Her neck bends awkwardly. In the moonlight her skin seems silver and blue and I have to hold her head up to make sure it stays attached to her body. She seems to quake, but I can't tell if it's me or her that is doing all the shaking.

"C'mon, Dawn," I say. I give her cheek a pat. I listen to her nose, for her whistley breath. "C'mon, Dawn. It's time to get up." But she doesn't have any whistley breath. She doesn't have any little noise coming from her nose or mouth at all. She doesn't have a thump in her heart or her neck. She doesn't move.

Something takes ahold of me. Angry as rapids.

"I said c'mon. We got to get home. Gram's gonna be worrying!" I shake her once, but she doesn't push me away like she usually does. I shake her again, harder this time. I shake her by her shirt's sleeves till she's swinging in my arms back and forth. A sharp pain fills my shoulder and my neck, and seems to explode into my head. The whole world swims in front of me, and the rapids fill my ears, and the coyotes are howling into the night. I join in with a high-pitched scream. I scream and scream, but my sister doesn't move. I drop her back in the sand and rocks, and my whole body moves like a machine.

"I said let's go!" I scream, and I can't help it, I punch Dawn right in the stomach. Hard. I punch her like I have never punched her before. Then just like that she curls up and starts puking on my arm. I have never been so happy to see Dawn puking, so I just start hanging on to her and I don't want to let her go, and so I sit there and rock her for a minute or two and hold her.

"I'm so sorry, Dawn. We never should've come. We never should've come."

Dawn shakes her head and looks at me. "Oh, Maple. The water. I—" I cut her off. Letting the tears flow now. Letting them pour down my cheeks onto her.

"Don't worry. Don't worry," I say.

She trembles in my arms.

"I'm tired, Maple," she says. "You gotta go get help or—" She expands in my arms and throws up again. "Something. I don't feel so good."

"Hang on, Dawn. You have to hang on!" I say.

I've never felt the way I do now; so tired I can hardly move, but moving faster than I ever have before. I tear out through the trees. I ignore the pain in my body, the howling in the night. I ignore everything except that feeling inside of me. I'm gonna get Dawn some help. Branches scrape my arms and legs. They hang on and pull at me, as though they're trying to hold me back. The earth under me is sharp and slippery, and I slide and scramble. One minute I'm on my feet and the next minute I'm climbing around on my hands and knees. I go up one hill and down another. Slide down the dead leaves. Over dead and rotting logs, into and over sharp barbed wire. I hit my toes on rocks and cut the bottoms of my feet on dry pine needles. I climb in and out of shadows.

Soon, I don't know how long I've been running—a day, a year? My eyes are getting foggy, and I'm not sure I'm going to make it. But I keep scrambling. The gauze that was wrapped around my hand is gone. Taken by the river. The cotton on my face, gone too, and I am open cuts and bruises. Branches grab my face. Twigs stick my palm. Everything tries to slow me. I tell myself to keep going, but I am like a toy running low on batteries. My legs are moving slower and slower and I fall on my knees and start crawling. And I search back and forth for something. For some sign of humans. And I grind to a halt and I know it's crazy, but right now I'm wishing I were a monarch because they are stronger than they look. And they're resilient. But mostly, like Mama says, they have intuition in their wings and they know how to get where they're going, and how to get home. And that's all I want right now, I want Dawn and me and the baby to get home. To get home to Mama and Papa and Beetle.

I tell myself to get up off my knees, but they tremble and shake and I can't stop myself from wondering if I am just heading farther into the woods. But I step forward.

And I fall against a tree and I look up, and though my eyes are blurring, I think that up ahead I see a glimmer. A little piece of orange light. And I smell something. Something strong and waxy, but sort of like dinner too. Something good cooking up. I run a hand across my eyes. And the whole scene comes clear. I step awkwardly through the trees. Pushing myself on. And when I realize I'm right, when I see the spooky smiling face of a jack-o'-lantern and then another and another, I break away running, straight for the pumpkin show. Straight for the Bee's Nest. Straight for the center of town.

"Help!" I scream. I reach out for them, and as I close in, the pumpkins blur, sneer, smile, collide into a mess of orange fire. A second later I trip and fall, but this time I scrape and slide across pavement, my knees caving in from the hit. I just want to lie there, but I can't. I have to move. I have to do this. I have to get help for Dawn. I'm here. I stand and look around. Across the street is the white gazebo and to my left is the Bee's Nest and to my right is Mr. Miller's carpentry shop. The glowing jack-o'-lanterns warm my side.

"Help!" I scream. "Help!" I run toward the Bee's Nest. Maybe Mr. Tinker is there putting on the morning coffee. I scream and bang on the door. Please, Mr. Tinker. Please be up.

I scream again. I scream until my voice is near

hoarse. Why is there nobody here watching the pumpkins? What time is it? Where is everyone? I knock until my knuckles bleed. I slide down the door and listen to the inside of the store. Listen for footsteps, for any sound.

"Maple, is that you?" A voice behind me barely whispers. I spin around. Mr. Miller is standing there. A flannel jacket is wrapped around his shoulders. And I see an abandoned lawn chair on the other side of the pumpkin stands. Mr. Miller is the one watching the pumpkins tonight. Mr. Miller is here. Mr. Miller can help. He takes off the flannel and rushes up the steps. "They've been looking everywhere for you. They've been—" He tries to wrap that flannel jacket around me.

"We've gotta, Dawn . . . Gotta help." I can't seem to get the words out. Can't seem to clear my head.

"Hang on," Mr. Miller says. He rushes away from me, and I try to stand. I lean against the railing and pull myself to my feet. There is no time to hang on. We have to move. We have to move.

"Yes, I need an ambulance right away."

"Mr. Miller—" I can hardly make out his figure, the pumpkins are so bright. The shiny metal of the pay phone blares like the center of a fire. The whole world looks orange. My eyes burn like someone has lit a candle behind them too. "Please, Mr. Miller, Dawn is . . .

Dawn's . . ." I teeter toward him, and he catches me in
his arms. "Out by the river."

"Maple, listen to me. Is she all right? Is she alive?
What happened?"

"She's alive," I tell him. "She's alive. Please, please,
please, p-p-plea—"

A siren screams in the distance. "You stay here, Maple.
Here comes the ambulance. I'll go and get Dawn. Stay
here."

Mr. Miller gets up and starts running out toward
the woods. Straight back the way I came. As the siren
draws closer, lights in all the nearby houses start to pop
on. The world seems filled with lights, too much light.
People come out into the street. Strange people touch me
and pick me up. Move me around. And I start losing it. I
start wondering things. I start feeling like I'm in a dream
and can't make myself wake up. I start thinking, *Where
is Dawn? Where am I?* I can't place how I got here. My
head is so full it feels like it could pop wide open. I feel
a tickle in my lungs and my teeth gnash in my head and
echo off one another. All the lights spin around me. The
jack-o'-lanterns grin, their bellies made of fire. They tilt
and rise and teeter, float in the air. But they can't do that,
can they? Where is Dawn? I search the parking lot, but
everything gets brighter and brighter and brighter. The
song of the *Cyanocitta cristata* echoes through the treetops.

But why would a blue jay be singing in the middle of the night?

"Dawn!" I scream. The lights in the pumpkin display seem to waver and dim. Their ghostly smiles grow darker and darker, until the world around me disappears.

Chapter Twenty-five

I wake in twisted sheets. It's dark and then light and then dark again and then light again, but eventually, darkness wins and I sink. Voices around me become deep and hollow and drift away like dandelion seeds on the spring breeze.

I want to follow.

Chapter Twenty-six

When I surface again, I'm pressed into sheets, snuggled up with someone warm and soft. Mama. Only her stomach is flat now, not filled to bursting. I shake in her arms and I feel them tighten around me. I don't want to open my eyes. Too many bad memories. I remember Dawn. I remember the day, the journey. I remember the baby. I remember the water, lost somewhere. Maybe I should just go back to sleep, maybe, for a little while longer. But Mama nudges me, and I peel my eyes open. The fluorescent lights of the hospital sting my eyes. It takes a moment before I can make out shapes and bodies.

Papa's draped across a chair, looking like a worn-out wool coat. Beetle sleeps across his lap. Her cheeks pink and rosy. Her helmet sits beside her, and she holds a tiny hand on top of the metal as though it were a soft teddy bear or blanket. Her thumb rests in her mouth, lips puffed out, sucking away.

Then there's Dawn, lying flat out in a hospital bed. And when I see her, I make myself calm down. She is beat up some, but she looks okay. She's bundled from head to toe with casts, but I see her chest moving up and down. And her cheeks are pink and looking much better than when I left her.

When I move, my body jerks against me. I feel like the Tin Man, but without my trusty oiling can. My right hand looks like a nest, wrapped and heavy with gauze. My shoulder feels strange. It's in the place it's meant to be, but it aches now all the same and it's wrapped with a sling. I reach up and feel a new bandage on my face. My cheek feels a little better, like there is no water under the skin. I examine my arms and legs. They're covered with gauze and bandages. Bruises: yellow, green, and blue ones pepper my skin. I sit up, but double over coughing. My throat feels like it's filled with burned cedar shavings, the ashes sliding into my lungs. I hack and cough, wishing I could somehow choke them out. But nothing comes up. They lodge uncomfortably in my throat. I feel Mama patting my back through the tremors and finally collapse back onto her arm. I don't remember a time when I had to try so hard just to breathe.

Mama clears her throat, and I hear her blow her nose. "You're lucky, you know," she says. I don't look at her eyes. I watch the ridges and valleys of the bed covers. Maybe I could sink into them. Disappear.

"You could have been killed. You and your sister both."

"How's Dawn?" I whisper.

"She's doing just fine, now anyway. That doesn't mean she won't be hurting for a while. You too."

I'm about to tell her I'm fine, but Mama starts up.

"Look at yourself. Sprained ankle, dislocated shoulder, a hand full of infection. Near hypotherm—" Mama's voice squeaks and she blows her nose again. "Look at you. And Dawn is worse off. She's got a broken leg, a sprained neck. Sprains all over. I don't know what happened to you two out there—" She pauses again and wipes her eyes.

"Mama—" I pat her leg with my good hand.

"I can't imagine ever losing you kids." She hiccups and blows her nose. Her voice gets higher and higher. "Don't want to even imagine. Now, I have been worried sick, Maple. I think you owe your mama an explanation."

My eyes must have been preparing for this moment, because they just start gushing, and as they do, I do too. I tell Mama everything. I tell her about sneaking into Papa's office, about getting the map in the night. About Dawn deciding to go with me. About going downriver with Curious. I tell her about the poachers. I tell her all about the fountain. I tell her about having the miracle in my hands, but about how it wasn't what I thought it would be, and I tell her about the truck and the river. I tell her about monarchs that are here out of season and about waking up to the northern lights. I tell her about bears that should be hunkering down for the winter, and a beaver out in the middle of the day. I tell her about it all until my throat goes dry and we have to call the nurse for a glass of water.

By the time I'm done, I can see Papa is awake too, and he's listening from the spot in his chair. He and Mama spend a lot of time looking back and forth at one another. Mama's eyes go from fierce to tender and soon she starts crying into her sheets. Then she says something about beavers and bears and butterflies aren't the only things that are going wild this season. And that I shouldn't just take up with wild ideas like the one that I had.

Papa says something about making rash decisions. He says that we should have talked to our parents about it before we just decided for ourselves that we were going to risk our own lives and limbs.

I let these words sink in, and I'm feeling a little bit humiliated because I know things would be different if I had the miracle water.

"But the water, Mama, it would have cured her," I say.

Mama wipes her eyes and looks over at Papa. Then she puts her arm around my shoulder and says, "There is no way to know, now, whether that water has the ability to grant miracles. In fact, Maple, maybe it does, or . . ." Mama pauses like she is afraid to say the next part. "Maybe it used to. Maybe the water shone like rose quartz and opal just as you imagined. But I think that perhaps the story of the Wise Woman of the Mountains isn't what it used to be."

I stop stock-still. "You mean, Mama, you don't think that water grants miracles? What about Remington. What about the stories?"

"I'm not saying it doesn't, Maple, but perhaps the miracle is altered with time. Perhaps it's a story that shows the miracles of nature. You know them, Maple, the designs of a spiderweb, the colors of autumn, the first fall of snow and the blue glow and silence that comes with it, the path of moonlight across open water."

I'm thinking I am a genuine dunce. Just like Dawn said, it was nothing but folklore.

"But Mama, what are we going to do? For the baby? I mean, if there isn't any miracle. What is there?"

"Well," Mama says, "there is medicine, there're good doctors, and there are loving sisters, and there is always hope."

This is the worst thing Mama has ever said. I know my mama to be smart, but something happens with brains when they get older. Something gets all fiddled around with so that they stop believing in fairies and ghosts and miracles too, I guess. But there is one thing I know: hope doesn't grant miracles, and neither do doctors or sisters. I cross my arms, wishing Dawn were awake, or Beetle. I look from one to the other and they're both clear into dreams.

"Can I go and see Lily, Mama?"

Mama pulls herself up a little bit and Mama and Papa look at each other again.

"I'll bring her," Papa says. He stands up and puts Beetle into Mama's arms. Beetle's eyes flutter open for a second and then she is out again. I give her a quick kiss on the cheek.

With Papa's help, I slide off the hospital bed and into a wheelchair. Papa puts a blanket over my lap and then he sweeps me down the hall. I see a lot of people here. There are kids and old people. People sitting outside hospital rooms and others walking the halls. I peek into rooms and see heads bowed and faces covered in tears, and in other rooms, people laughing and holding their bellies like something is hilarious. We swing over blue and white tiles. We follow yellow lines along the floor until we pull up to a window in the wall. The door next to the window says NICU.

I look in. Babies. I count eight. Eight babies trying to survive. Babies with little suction cups sticking all over them. Some have baby oxygen masks over their mouths and noses. They're tiny and they look strange, like tadpoles that have started becoming frogs but are stuck in the awkward place in between. They're each in their own tub. They're each all alone. My stomach does a flip and I put my head in my hand.

"There she is. There's Lily." Papa leans over and puts his finger to the glass. "She looks just like a Rittle, doesn't she?" Papa says.

I nod even though I am not quite sure. I lean into the glass so my face is nearly pressed up against it. She is tiny and her eyes are closed and she isn't squirming, not like a strong, healthy baby should.

"Can we go in, Papa?" I ask, making a fog smear across the window.

"Sorry, kiddo. Germs. Your little sister is very sensitive right now, and you're sick yourself."

Papa's voice sinks at the end of his sentences and

when I look at him, I notice the big circles around his eyes. He looks so worn and weak, like maybe he took a trip downriver himself. "But," Papa says, "you can sit here and watch over her as long as you want."

"Will she be okay?" I say.

Papa pauses and stares at the floor. His breath is coming raggedy and he won't look me in the face. It's in that long pause that I get to knowing what he is thinking.

"I hope so," he says after a while. "But Maple, I'm not so sure and I don't think it is fair, either, that you should have to even see this at your age, but we're here now and you have to face the truth of the matter just like your papa. If her heart doesn't get stronger, she's not going to make it through the week." Papa's voice fades into a whisper and his gaze dwindles with the words and I know I have failed him and Lily, and Mama and Dawn and Beetle.

"How can we make her heart stronger?" I ask him.

"Well, Maple, we can't make her heart stronger. The nurses can monitor it, though, and they can let us know if anything changes. See that little box next to your sister?"

I look into the room again and I see the green box with its wiry arms and suction-cup hands that stick out onto my sister.

"That green line jumps every time your sister's heart

pumps. Right now, it's less of a thump, more like a blip. But over time, I hope that that bump gets a little bit stronger, more frequent."

Papa clears his throat. "You ready to go and see Dawn? She may be up and about."

"No, Papa, I don't want to leave Lily," I say, putting my hand on his shoulder.

He nods. "I'll be back to check on you in a minute, then."

So I sit there, feeling heavy, 'cause I got no answers left. I lost the miracle. I could try and escape to go and get it again, but I don't think I'd get very far the way I am busted up. And then what if it didn't work? What if it was like Dawn says and gives Lily giardia instead of a miracle? So I'm trying to find something within my reach. I sit there almost the entire day. And the sunset starts reaching in the window, looking golden and beautiful. I look down the hallway toward it 'cause it's my favorite time of day, and there is a monarch. It's sitting there on the window ledge. I look at my sister in the NICU and I look out at the butterfly. And I start thinking on butterflies and their fragile wings and what Mama said about them having a better chance of survival together. I start wondering if Lily is like the monarch; maybe she isn't as fragile as she looks, but all the same, she would be better off with other butterflies. If only I could make her heart stronger, give her some muscles of my own. It's as I'm sitting there thinking this that Papa wheels Dawn up next to me, and there we are, just a couple of wounded soldiers with nothing to show for it.

I hear Papa's footsteps recede down the hallway and Dawn's hand slides across the wheelchair and she clasps my hand.

"Mama was wrong, Maple."

"Huh?" I say.

"I was listening to you talking to Mama in there. You were right all along, about there being a miracle, I mean. It was the last verse. That was our mistake, Maple. We forgot the last verse," she says.

"The last verse?" I say, not sure right away what she is talking about.

"In the folk song. After you came down here, Mama started singing it and I started thinking about the inscription. 'Read and understand,' do you remember? It was the verse inscribed in the fountain. We read it all wrong."

I never remember the last verse of the song. Mama had sung it for me, but we hadn't sung it together many times, not like the other verses. I start thinking of the fountain and Dawn's hand sliding under the algae and the chopped-up words and letters and then Mama's voice lilts in my ear and I remember the verse like it's part of me, like it was there all along, just hiding in one of my brain crevices. I start to sing, and Dawn's voice joins mine:

> *Water, sun, moon, and rain*
> *Will do their part to heal.*
> *Still greater powers come to call*
> *When love brings strength, concealed.*

> *Love and love, the purest love*
> *Heals the wounds of man.*
> *Love and love, the purest love*
> *Is miracle in hand . . .*

I squeeze Dawn's hand, and we each lean our heads up against the glass, trying not to smear too much, and we send all our love straight through the wall, 'cause not even a solid wall can stop that coming through . . . and just a second later, there is Lily, turning her face to look at us, and her eyes open, and they are Rittle-sister blue, bright and clear. Her heart monitor skips, and for a minute I think we failed again, but a second later it jumps again and then again and again, and the nurse is getting curious. She calls the other nurses over to the baby, and she grabs her clipboard, and my heart, I feel it pumping too, almost like those wiry heart-monitor arms are linked right up to me. *Bomp bomp bomp.*

One nurse smiles at the other nurse and Lily is still

looking at Dawn and me with her big blue eyes and I smile at her and put my other hand up against the glass. The nurses are all talking to one another and the head nurse is checking things off on her clipboard with her shiny pen. They are nodding their heads and patting each other on the back, because right then and there Lily turns the corner.

Chapter Twenty-seven

Two days later, Gramma comes to pick us up. I have been to visit Lily every day. She seems to be doing all right. The same day as our visit to the NICU, the doctor told Mama and Papa that Lily was going to make it. They're still a little sore at us, but they're smiling more often.

"Bye, Lily," I say as I look at her through the NICU window. "I'll be back soon, but right now I gotta get home."

I wave to my baby sister. Then Papa wheels me to the lobby.

"Dress the bandages daily," Nurse Jane says to

Gramma, and hands her a long list. She shows Gramma how to adjust the sling on my arm. "They should both take plenty of time to rest. No running around."

"Don't worry about that," Gramma says. "They'll be lucky if I let them leave the couch." She looks sideways at me and I look down at the tiles.

"They both got quite a chill out there. Luckily the worst is over. Give them plenty of vitamin C. Stop at the pharmacy on the way home." She hands Gramma another white sheet of paper. Then Nurse Jane pulls Dawn over in a wheelchair. Dawn has more bandages than me, but she's doing all right. She's even ordered me around a little bit: "Go get me some of that red Jell-O" and "Go check on the baby."

Gramma puts Beetle on my lap and wheels us out to the car with the help of Nurse Jane. She packs us in the back of the station wagon. The plastic maroon seats squeak as we adjust ourselves. Gramma fusses with our buckles, unclipping them and then clipping them again. Finally, she gets into the front seat and tilts the mirror so it's pointing straight at me. I look out the window as we pull onto the road.

We make our way home, and knowing that has never felt so good. I just sit back and try to watch the scenery, but Gramma eyes me a lot in the mirror, like she's not sure if I'll spring out of the backseat or not. She pulls a tissue out of her sleeve and wipes her nose every once in a while, then looks at me again.

Beetle plays with my hair from her baby seat, and sometimes she drops her toys, which I have to lean down and pick up, but I snuggle her a little extra all the same. I look over to Dawn, who is resting her head on the back of her seat. Her eyes are closed, but as soon as we hit the dirt road, her face opens with a smile.

Three miles running along the river, out past Mr. Benny's apple orchard, and over the hill from Nanny Ann's farm stand, and we're home. Three bumps as we spin into the dirt driveway. The house pops out against bare trees. The car thumps to a halt and Gramma gets out of her seat.

"Maple. You first, please," she says as she opens my door. She undoes my buckle and I step gingerly onto the driveway. My ankles are sore and my knees are stiff, but I can walk. She puts an arm around my waist and helps me up the stairs and through the door. Curious comes spinning around the corner as soon as we walk in.

According to Papa, he did end up with the Collinses for the whole day. And I pity him for that. As soon as he sees me, he wants to jump up on me, but then he sits back on his heels and looks at the scene. His ears perk up and his head tilts to the side and it's the look of genuine concern from a genuine friend. I pat his head

and give his chin a scrub. He licks my hand and puts his
paw right up over my wrist. Gramma helps me to the
couch. I sit and Curious runs off upstairs. A second later,
I hear his collar jangling and he has come down with
Paddington Bear nestled gently in his teeth. I take the old
bear from his mouth.

"Thanks, Curio," I say, feeling Paddington's soft fur.

Gramma walks through the door carrying Beetle.
"Here, Maple, can you manage Beetle while I get Dawn?"
she says as she plops Beetle down on my lap. I hold
her with my good arm and she points at things out the
window. Curious lies down at my feet and a few min-
utes later, Gramma eases Dawn onto the couch. There
we are, sitting around like baby mice trying to stay safe
and warm.

Gramma goes off into the kitchen, muttering and
wiping her nose. "It's a miracle," she mutters. She walks
in and out of the living room and kitchen like she's on
patrol. Soon, I'm seeing the sun setting in the yard and
I ask Gramma if we can sit outside to watch the world
turn golden. Course, she says yes, and we all hobble out
on the porch like kids from a plane wreck. Gramma
plants herself right at the door with a chair and she pulls
out some knitting.

The day is warm, even here with the sun sinking. I sit
on the top step. Beetle climbs into my lap and sits right

down on my sore arm. Dawn sits with her back against mine, and we gaze out at the grass and soak up the last of autumn's rays. I suspect Dawn is thinking about Lily. I know I am.

I'm watching the leaves chase each other around the yard, when out of nowhere four monarchs flit across the lawn. They should all be gone, so I know something is out of the ordinary. It almost seems as though a few came back for the one that was left behind. But now, together, they head south across the yard, over the river, and into the trees, and I'm feeling good about the survival of each and every one. Together, they are a genuine miracle.

ACKNOWLEDGMENTS

There are so many people to thank for the completion of this book. First and foremost, I would like to thank Ellen Howard for seeing what I needed and imploring me to write what I know. It was studying with you that I first found Maple and her story. I would like to thank the entire faculty and staff at Vermont College, especially those advisors that worked on this piece during workshop: Cynthia Leitich Smith and Jane Kurtz. Thank you, also, to my classmates, who are always a source of knowledge and inspiration. I would like to give a hearty thanks to Kathi Appelt, a great mentor and friend who pushed me through the later drafts with love and encouragement.

Many thanks to my critique partners, Trinity Peacock-

Broyles, Tamara Ellis Smith, Cindy Faughnan and especially Kerry Castano for the multiple readings of this book. Kerry, your guided editorial eye brought this book to where it is. In addition, I would like to thank Helen Hemphill for her generous reading and comments in the later drafts of this piece.

Thank you to my amazing agent, Ammi-Joan Paquette, for believing in me and representing me. And thank you for the ending that I just couldn't seem to find. Thank you also to all the brilliant staff at the Erin Murphy Literary Agency. Thanks to my editor, Jill Santopolo, for making this story and dream real.

Thanks to my family. After all, *it all starts at home, on the mountain.* Thank you for the mountain, for an unparalleled childhood, and for fostering love, imagination, knowledge, wisdom and strength.

And most importantly, thank you to Howie, who never ceases to make me smile and write and love.

Turn the page for a sample of
Erin E. Moulton's next book . . .

Chapter 1

I DROP LOW IN THE SEAT and look out the bus window. We pass Pa's shop, Chickory and Chips Famous Fishery. I wave to the wooden pirate, Barnacle Briggs, who is always out front holding the shop sign. We zip on past and turn right onto Blue Jay Crossing. I hold my backpack on my lap. It shifts back and forth as the bus jostles over the bumpy road.

It's the last day of school. The last day of fifth grade and I'm dying for it to be over. I make a fish face in the window as we pass the harbor where Pa's boat, the *Mary Grace,* usually sits. The spot is empty 'cause he's already out making his rounds. Pa is the best fisherman in all of Plumtown and brings in the most lobsters. But that's not all. He dredges for mussels and also catches hake, fluke, flounder, monkfish, whiting, ocean perch, pollack, and sometimes wolffish. Wolffish is the ugliest fish I've ever seen, but it tastes all right if you ask me. I make the face of a wolffish in the window, pulling my mouth down into a big line from one side of my chin to the other. I pop my eyes way out and pull my eyebrows down into the middle the best I can and I think it's a pretty great wolffish grin. Real menacing and gross.

"*Indie.*" I look away from my reflection and over to my older sister, Bebe, in the seat across from me. "Stop it," she says out of the corner of her mouth. She doesn't like it when I make fish faces anymore, even though she used to love it. Now she's too old and mature for that sort of thing, and whenever I do it, she pretty much pretends she doesn't know me.

I throw on a trout pout because that's the one she used to giggle at the most, but this time she groans and looks out her window.

My backpack almost slides off my lap and I grab at it. Then the bus squeals to a stop and a whole bunch of kids get on at The Manors. That's the cul-de-sac where all the rich people live. Mom says you don't move to Plumtown unless you're rich or you're a hard worker. That's the way it goes. We're in the hard-worker part. I make sure to scrunch way over in case any of the fancy kids want to have a seat, but as usual, I can spread out, 'cause three kids all cram into the seat in front of me and one sits down right next to Bebe and they start talking like they're best pals.

We go around and take a right onto Main Street, and as the breeze blows in from the open window in the seat in front of me, I can smell the mix of sugar and salt from Sandy's Saltwater Candies. I basically start drooling thinking of that delicious blue raspberry flavor. I lick my lips and consider walking home today 'cause it's about that time of year where Mrs. Callypso will be standing out with free samples. When the bus stops again, I stay scrunched over, but Lynn and June, who get on at the last stop, go by my seat and make crinkling faces.

"You stink, Indie," June says.

I can see Bebe roll her eyes across the way.

"Sorry," I say, smelling my fingers, wondering if they stink of herring from feeding The Lobster Monty Cola this morning. Herring is one of his favorite snacks. He also likes fish heads that have been sitting out for a while, and my hand might have brushed past that, too. But I don't mind if it stinks a little. The Lobster Monty Cola is my best pal besides Bebe. And even a better pal now that Bebe got all perfect and can't stand me anymore. Monty's not some ordinary crustacean; he's a golden lobster. Pa says you come across one golden lobster in every 30 million lobsters you trap. And he got Monty in a real amazing catch. Now Monty lives in a saltwater pool outside my window, and if he wants some herring and some fish heads, well, that's what he is going to get.

"Oh, seriously," Lynn says. As she passes, she pulls her shirt up over her nose. I push my hand underneath my leg, hoping that might help bury the smell.

June and Lynn sit down together over in the last seat. It's really a half seat, meant for one person, but that's where they sit. I pretend like that doesn't bother me a bit. I hum a little and look out the window and watch the joggers go up and down the boardwalk. A minute later, the brakes squeak and we're in front of Plumtown Elementary.

"Happy last day!" Mrs. McKowski says as she opens the door. Mrs. McKowski is one of the people in the hard-worker portion, too. She has driven the bus since I started in kindergarten. I swing my backpack on and stand up to get off. Every time I try to get into the line, someone else gets there first, so I wait until the very last kid has gone, then I go, too.

"See you at pickup, Indie," Mrs. McKowski says.

"Bye, Mrs. McKowski." I walk in past the giant sailor sculptures and trot along behind Bebe into Mr. Lemur's class.

Chapter 2

I WATCH THE CLOCK for most of the morning, wishing that the day would zip by just a little faster. I want to get home, relax, then go to Templeton's for ice cream. Mom and Pa bring us there every year on the very last day of school, plus days in between, but the last day of school is especially great 'cause they make Colossal Creemees for dirt cheap. That's what the sign says and that's what they do. I watch the hands on the clock tick along, thinking about what flavor I might get. Finally, lunchtime comes around and I grab a seat as quick as I can and pull out the container of lobster bisque Mom sent. The best thing about Pa being a great fisherman and owning Chickory and Chips is that we get the best meals. Mrs. Barkley works at Chickory and Chips and she makes the best lobster bisque I've ever tasted. Even though Mom develops the recipes, Mrs. Barkley runs the shop and lots of the time we have the leftovers for lunch. I unscrew the top of my thermos and pour some of the bisque into it.

A few kids pass by and I wave to Bebe, letting her know that there's a seat open right across from me if she wants it, but just as she gets up close, she veers off to the right. Marty Shanks, a kid with a mullet, sits across from me. Great. Whenever Marty sits with me, my food never tastes quite as good as it usually does. I watch a couple crumbs fall off his lips as he bites into his salami and mayonnaise sandwich, and I can't help making a monkfish face. He spots me looking at him, ducks his head down and holds his sandwich up over his mouth like he doesn't see me. Still, I can see his mangled teeth through the spaces between his fingers and they're grinding his food into mash. And between that and the cafeteria smelling like cartons of milk, my stomach gets a little choppy, like the waves before a storm.

I look over at Bebe, but the seat right next to her and the one across from her are full, so I eat my lobster bisque quickly, trying not to look at Marty. I just focus on my spoon going up and down and that's it. Then I head back to the cloakroom. As I unzip my backpack to put my lunch box away, something weird happens. My backpack shifts the teensiest little bit. I let go of it and stand back. It shifts again, and a crusher claw floats up at me from the bottom. A golden crusher claw.

"Monty!" I say, and pull the backpack open. I stare in, not believing my eyes. What is he doing here? Monty waves his claw at me and clip-claps it in front of my face. He looks like he's about to climb out. Kathy McCue comes in and I slap his claw down and step in front of my backpack so I'm between her and Monty. She goes to her fancy purple backpack, then her nose starts moving up and down like a bloodhound on a scent.

"Indie Lee Chickory, you stink like the salt sea," she says, dropping her lunch box into her pack and pinching her nose. She sticks her tongue out at the same time. Well, she's not the only one who can make a stink face. I think for a minute if I want to do the puffer or the mackerel, or if I should do the pinched shrimp or the wide whale. In the end I know the trout pout is the one that will really get her. I frown, cross my eyes and suck in my cheeks. Then, for added effect, I make a groaning sound in the back of my throat. It's perfect for the job.

"Stupid weirdo," she says, and heads out of the cloak-room.

Nice work, I think as I unscrew my face and check the doorway to see if any others are coming in. It seems pretty empty, so I look back down at my pack and peer into the bottom.

"Monty Cola, how could you?" I whisper, pulling him up out of the dark and laying him across my arm. I check his forehead for dampness, because one thing I know about lobsters is that they're okay without water if they stay good and damp. But if he was in my backpack, that means he must have climbed in when I brought him the herring this morning. Which means that he's been in there for a solid three hours or more. Plus, he'll have to wait until the end of the school day to get back in his pool, and that seems like forever from now.

"Not a good plan, Monty, not a good plan at all!" I say. I don't mean to be harsh, but Monty Cola thinks he can survive anything, outsmart anybody. He basically thinks he's invincible.

"Time to line up for recess!" Mr. Lemur hollers from the other room. I listen as the kids thunder toward the door. I look down at The Lobster Monty Cola and he looks at me and draws his little antennas around and around in circles.

If only I could just sneak him out and run up the street to Crawdad Beach.

"Has anyone seen Indie?" Mr. Lemur says. Dang Mr. Lemur! He's too good at keeping an eye on everyone. I crane my neck and can barely see the kids lining up at the door.

"Bebe, can you check the cloakroom?" Mr. Lemur says.

"Sure," Bebe says, real quiet. Bebe's one grade older than me, but it doesn't matter in Plumtown 'cause most of our classes are multi-age. We're in fifth/sixth with Mr. Lemur.

I turn so my arms and Monty are tucked a little bit behind my backpack. A second later Bebe walks into the cloakroom, her ponytail bouncing and her white shorts basically blinding me.

"What are you doing?" she says, flipping her silky-smooth bangs behind her ear.

"Nothing. Be right there," I say, tucking my snarly hair behind my ear with my right hand. I make an extra show of it, to keep her eyes up, not down where Monty Cola is starting to squirm around on my forearm.

I curl in, trying to hide the movement, but Bebe eyes me and just like that, she spots him. I don't know if it's his antenna or his leg or his pincher, but she spots him.

"You have got to be kidding." She crosses her arms and stalks over to me, putting on what looks a lot like a trout pout. Not that she would admit it.

"Listen—it was an accident," I say.

"What is wrong with you?" she hisses.

"He snuck into my bag," I say as Monty starts wiggling around on my arm. I pat his head, trying to calm him down a bit.

"Put him back, then," she says.

I scowl at her because she obviously doesn't care if Monty Cola lives or dies. But I can see from her jaw clenching so tight that she isn't going to let this drop.

"Is she in there, Bebe?" Mr. Lemur calls from the other room.

"Yes, coming!" we say at the same time.

"Okay, okay, I'll put him back," I whisper, and pretend like I am putting him in my backpack.

Bebe nods and then leaves. And I pull him out. Of

course I'm not going to put Monty in my backpack again. I'm not some sort of heartless animal.

"I'm not leaving you here, Monty Cola. Hang tight," I whisper. I look all around the cloakroom, wondering if Mr. Lemur would notice if I have my backpack with me for recess. Probably. He's pretty smart about that sort of thing. Maybe I could make a quick escape. I look from ceiling to floor and wall to wall, but there's no window in here. I give the floor a stomp. It's really solid wood.

"That's not our best bet, Monty," I say. It would take days, maybe even years to dig us out of here. I lick my lips. C'mon, think, think.

"Indie!" Mr. Lemur says.

That's when I look down at my plaid button-up.

"All right, Monty. You've got to play dead. Got it?"

Monty lifts his pincher claw and clip-claps it twice. That usually means "yes," so I lift my shirt and push him up, then tuck the bottom of my shirt into my Carhartts so he is in a sort of pouch. I feel him curl his legs up against himself. I take a quick peek down to make sure that the buttons are not popping. It looks pretty good, pretty natural. So I saunter out into the classroom and get in line.

"All right, let's try that a little faster at the last bell, okay?"

I nod and put my eyes on the back of my sister's shiny

hair as we go down the stairs. As soon as we swing out the front door and the smell of the sea comes rolling along on the breeze, Monty starts to wiggle a little.

"Hang on, Monty," I whisper. "We'll be going for a quick dunk soon."